This book belongs to:

gordon
....

Donaldson
....

MY BOOK OF Funny STORIES

MY BOOK OF Funny STORIES

Written by
NICOLA BAXTER

Illustrated by
SASCHA LIPSCOMB

This is a Parragon Book
First published in 2000

Parragon
Queen Street House
4 Queen Street
Bath BA1 1HE, UK

ISBN 0-75253-668-0

Produced for Parragon by
Nicola Baxter
PO Box 215
Framingham Earl
Norwich NR14 7UR

Designed by Amanda Hawkes

Printed in Italy

Contents

Aunt Monica's Knickers

Ben and Bea were twins. On their own they were no naughtier than any seven-year-olds, but somehow when they got together it was a different story. Neither of them wanted to seem more scared or more serious than the other. And, of course, Angel didn't help.

Angel was the twins' cousin, but she had lived with her aunt and uncle since before the twins were born. Although she loved her cousins *most* of the time, she had never quite forgotten how their arrival had changed her life. Where once she had been the *only* child in the house, suddenly she was the eldest of three. Worse than that, because she was four years older, she often had to *help* with the demanding babies. Angel had a strong feeling that things had been a good deal better before two red and crying creatures had suddenly appeared. She did suggest in the nicest possible way to her aunt and uncle that the babies were sent straight back to where they had come from. Disappointingly, from Angel's point of view, neither Uncle Mike nor Aunt Sonia had seemed enthusiastic about the idea.

Angel sulked for a year or two. (She was a champion sulker!) Then, as the twins became toddling trouble-makers, she suddenly realized that it could be fun to encourage them in their naughtiness.

When the twins had done something truly dreadful, Angel found herself in her aunt's and uncle's good books once again.

"At least you understand what I'm saying to you," Aunt Sonia would say, giving Angel a hug. "Did I or did I not quite clearly tell those two *not* to pull the tablecloth?"

"You did, Aunty," Angel would reply with a look of wide-eyed innocence. She omitted to tell her aunt that she had herself reversed this instruction when talking to the twins a few minutes later.

As the twins grew up, they got into trouble more often than you would think possible. It was quite easy for them to fit in at least five dreadful deeds between breakfast and supper. At least half of these were in some way encouraged by Angel, even if all she did was to turn the other way when something naughty was going on. Now that both she and the twins were older, she was very often asked to stay in the same room and just keep an eye on them while her aunt prepared lunch or made some phone calls.

When it comes to the whole hilarious business of Aunt Monica's knickers, Angel must take some of the blame. It was Angel, you see, who suggested the idea of the scavenger hunt.

"What's a savage hunt?" asked Ben, already wondering if he could wear his tiger mask for it.

"Not *savage, scavenger,*" said Angel. "It's a kind of competition. You have a list of things you have to find and bring back to the start. The first one to do it is the winner."

"What sort of things?" asked Bea. "We're not allowed to go out of the garden, you know."

"It doesn't matter," said Angel. "They can be things like a feather, or a candle, or an old toothbrush."

Bea and Ben had left the room before she finished speaking.

"Those were just examples!" called Angel, but it was no good. Once the twins got an idea into their heads, they didn't give up. Fifteen minutes later, the pair reappeared clutching half of their mother's feather duster, a candle in the shape of a snowman, and an old toothbrush that had obviously been used to clean shoes. Large streaks of boot polish had transferred themselves to Ben's face. Bea appeared to be covered in some kind of white powder.

"We found them! We found them!" cried Ben.

"That's brilliant!" said Angel, and she was genuinely impressed. "I wouldn't have thought of the feather duster. But where did you find these other things?"

A scream of horror from the hallway showed that someone at least had discovered the full enthusiasm with which the twins had searched.

In spite of all the clearing up to do later, under their mother's watchful eye, the twins were keen to have another go at a scavenger hunt. It was exciting and if they were careful, they thought, it might not be so obvious that they were forced to ransack the house to find things. Angel promised to give it some thought.

It was at just this time that Aunt Monica came to stay. She was not, in fact, the twins' aunt at all, but their father's aunt. She was a woman who, although she had no children of her own, had very strict views on how they should be brought up. Within seconds of her arrival, the twins' mother was already clutching the doorknob with unusual force.

"Hello, my dear," were Aunt Monica's opening words. "Are these the twins? My goodness, how they've grown. Do you really think it is wise to let them

run about barefoot? There are so many dangers, even in a very clean and tidy house, and I don't think we can say that this one comes under *that* category."

Aunt Monica gave a little laugh, to show that it was a joke, but the twins' mother's returning smile lacked warmth.

"They are fine like that indoors," she said. "Let me take your bag. Ooof! This is very heavy. You look as if you've come for months!"

Even the twins noticed that there was a desperate note in their mother's own laugh. Aunt Monica beamed broadly.

"Well, after that terrible flood, it is going to take a long time to get my house back in order. Of course, I worry about how the repair men are getting on, and they may take longer if I'm not there, but it is so distressing to someone as sensitive as I am to see all the mess and disorder. I am much better to stay here while all the work is done. It shouldn't take more than a few months."

"A few months?" Mrs. Mark leaned against the wall and felt a little faint. "We thought you were coming for the weekend. We really don't have much room here, you know."

"I'm happy to sleep anywhere," cried Aunt Monica magnanimously. "Of course, I will need a room to myself. It needs to be not too far from the bathroom. And it would be better if it was towards the back of the house, so that the traffic doesn't disturb me. I am a very light sleeper, I'm afraid. And after everything I've been through..."

Mrs. Mark turned to see Angel, who had heard every word, emerging from the sitting room with a cold look in her eyes.

"I'm sorry, Angel," said her aunt, "but it sounds as if your room would be perfect. I know you won't mind moving in with the twins for ... er ... a week or two, will you?"

Angel smiled with her mouth, but her eyes were stony.

"Of course not, Aunt Sonia," she said, in a tone that made shivers run up and down her aunt's spine. "I'll go and start moving my things now."

"What a well-behaved child," beamed Aunt Monica. "Rather a contrast to your own two, Sonia, I must say.

Bea and Ben were busy stalking the cat as it slunk down the hallway.

"We think of Angel as one of our own," said Sonia Mark firmly. "And yes, she is a good girl, but then she is four years older than the twins. Now, let me see if I can manage to get your bag up the stairs for you."

After the effort of dragging the bag upstairs and helping a very silent Angel to move her things, Mrs. Mark felt the need to sit down with a cool drink. It was not to be.

"I've been travelling since half-past seven this morning," said Aunt Monica. "I do feel as if I may faint if I don't have a little snack soon. Just something simple will be fine. An omelette perhaps, with a green salad and a little fruit or cheese to follow. I'll go and sit down, shall I, so that I don't get in your way in your rather, well, *snug* kitchen?"

Aunt Monica made herself at home while the twins' mother hurried off to make the snack. She was pretty sure that all the eggs had been eaten at breakfast and a trip to the corner store would be needed.

"I may have to pop out for a moment," she said. "Could you just keep an eye on the children while I go? I'll only be five minutes."

It might have been five years for all the fuss Aunt Monica made, but Mrs. Mark felt she had no choice but to leave in the middle of her visitor's explanation about her fragile nerves.

By the end of the first day, when Aunt Monica had used all the hot water (to soothe her rheumatism), pushed away her supper (and suggested that perhaps a small portion of chicken could be prepared for her instead), and criticized the way the twins ate, talked, played and looked at her (they had already made up their minds that Aunt Monica was not their favourite person in the world), the family went to bed exhausted and frayed.

While Mr. and Mrs. Mark bickered in their bedroom, Angel sat on the spare bed in the twins' room and thought long and hard. She had quite distinctly heard the word "months" being used about the old lady's stay. It was, Angel decided, much, much too long. But how on earth could she make sure Aunt Monica left earlier than planned?

It wasn't until the next morning that Angel came up with her plan. She had noticed that Aunt Monica liked things to be *very* neat and tidy. She saw that Aunt Monica had brought lots of little pots of face cream and powders and arranged them neatly on the dressing table in her (Angel's) room. Finally, Angel saw Aunt Monica's knickers which, together with some other items of clothing, had been given to Mrs. Marks with the thought that it would be best if they were washed right away. The knickers were enormous! Angel couldn't resist calling the twins to look out of the window at the washing blowing on the line. Their fits of giggles lasted all through lunch, mystifying and annoying Aunt Monica, who gave Mrs. Mark the benefit of some more of her advice on child-rearing.

Later that day, Angel beckoned the twins into the garden. They all crouched in the treehouse, where she gave her cousins a piece of paper.

"I've written another scavenger hunt," she said. "These things have to be brought to me by suppertime tomorrow. Okay?"

The twins were excited. The list looked difficult, but they were eager to start at once. This is what it looked like.

SCAVENGER HUNT

1. An eggshell full of lavender-scented face cream.

2. Twelve grey hairs.

3. A red button.

4. A pair of super-sized knickers.

"Are you aware," Aunt Monica asked the twins' mother next morning, "that your children appear to be looking for food in the dustbin? I must say, I'm not surprised they were hungry after eating that inadequate chocolate cereal at breakfast. A child's nutritional needs are very complex, my dear."

Mrs. Mark was a little short with her visitor as she hurried to extract her youngsters from the rubbish. But when she emerged from the kitchen door, they had already disappeared, leaving a trail of empty cans and potato peelings behind them. It didn't help that Aunt Monica,

still in mid flow about vitamins and minerals, came out behind her and slipped over on a cabbage leaf.

Aunt Monica frightened Mrs. Mark badly by lying on the ground and moaning for a very long time. She was just about to call for an ambulance when Aunt Monica scrambled to her feet, said she needed to lie down, and hurried up to her room. The squawk of rage she let out when she saw the spilt powders and creams all over her dressing table could be heard five streets away. Aunt Monica retired to the sitting room to rest while Mrs. Mark cleared up.

But there was no rest for Aunt Monica. Each time she closed her eyes, she heard giggling and felt a sharp pain in her head. It was almost as if someone was pulling her hair out, strand by strand. Aunt Monica decided that the shock of her fall had been greater than she thought. It was only when the twins got bored and decided to yank out several hairs at once that Aunt Monica caught them.

The outraged visitor marched straight to her hostess and began again on one of her talks about discipline and control of small children. She spoke warmly about what kind of people children who tortured old people became.

She foresaw a dark future for Bea and Ben, mostly spent in institutions of one kind or another. She begged Mrs. Mark to get them psychiatric help right away and, to show that she did her best to sympathize with the unfortunate, went so far as to lay her hand on her hostess's arm and tell her she would be thinking of her as she faced the difficult years ahead.

It was too much for Mrs. Mark. She delivered herself of a few sharp remarks about people who talked about things they knew nothing about. She admitted that children should not try to pull out other people's hair but said that she really felt they should find out *why* they had attempted such an extraordinary act before assuming that they were budding psychopaths.

Aunt Monica sniffed and marched out of the room.

"I know where I'm not wanted," she said. "I shall start packing at once. Perhaps you would be so good as to call me a taxi."

Mrs. Mark, filled with guilt, made a half-hearted attempt to get her visitor to change her mind. Then, with relief, she rang for the taxi.

Aunt Monica seemed to take a very long time to do her packing. She was found roaming around the house in a vague way, looking under cushions. When the taxi arrived, she confronted the twins.

Aunt Monica seemed a little flushed. "The fact is," she said, trying to look stern, "I've lost something, and I have reason to believe that you two are responsible."

"Who, us?" chorused Ben and Bea, giving looks of such wide-eyed innocence that their mother knew there and then they were definitely guilty of *something.*

"What have you lost?" asked Bea with her sweetest smile.

Aunt Monica opened her mouth and shut it again. Somehow, she just could not bring herself to go on. She marched out of the gate and into the taxi—luckily for all concerned, she didn't look back.

Doug, the Dreadful Dog

My dog Doug is great in almost every way. He knows I'm boss, for one thing. If Mum says, "Down, Doug!" he jumps up higher and plants two big muddy pawprints in embarrassing places on her jumper. If Dad says, "Good boy, Doug, sit!" Doug runs round and round until the lead is wrapped all the way up Dad's legs and he can't move without falling over. No, from that point of view, Doug is perfect. He only listens to me, and he obeys me at once. When I say, "Sit!" he sits. When I say "Down!" he gets down and looks up with his big brown eyes.

There's only one thing he doesn't pay attention about, and it's really rather embarrassing. You see, Doug has never got the hang of lampposts. He likes to … er … visit bicycles, doorsteps, buses, car tyres and, I'm sorry to say, legs, especially blue ones. No policeman, postman or plumber is safe from Doug, and not surprisingly, they don't like it. I can't blame them at all. Nowadays, anyone who *knows* Doug breaks into a run when he comes into view. Those who don't are in for a bit of a surprise.

Doug started his little habit when he was just a puppy. I blame Mum. She was keen to train him as soon as possible not to leave little puddles in the house. Her keenness became even stronger when she sleepily crawled out of bed one day and found that her slippers were strangely damp inside.

For several days, Mum took Doug outside at regular intervals and waited patiently with chocolate drops for him to do what he had to do. It took ages. Mum got so bored she took a book with her and then missed any activity there might have been. All this time, what Doug really needed was to see what other dogs did. It finally happened early one Wednesday morning. Mum was outside in the garden, still in her dressing gown, pacing up and down the path, when the postman arrived with a couple of parcels.

"Everything all right, Mrs. W.?" he asked. "Not locked yourself out again?"

This was something that Mum had a habit of doing. Usually, she locked herself out of the car, but she had been known to have to break into the house as well after dropping the keys down a drain.

"No, no," said Mum on this occasion. "I'm just waiting for Doug here to do his business. So far, he's never once done it outside. It's always in the house. It's getting to be more than I can stand."

Who knows why, at just that moment, Doug decided to grow up at last. He looked for the nearest tall object, saw two lanky blue legs and ... well ... you can imagine what happened next.

"Eeeeeaaaagh!" cried the postman.

"Good boy, Doug!" cried Mum, liberally dishing out chocolate drops.

Well, that was that. Doug learnt his lesson well, it just wasn't the right lesson. Mum protested that he should have known she didn't mean that using legs as lampposts was okay, but he was, after all, only a little dog at the time.

"Anyway," said Mum heartlessly, "as long as he doesn't do it on *my* legs, I don't mind. It's a hazard of the job for postmen and the like. It would be much worse if he *bit* them. They should be grateful. Anyway, he's only small. It's not as if they're drenched or anything."

"He'll grow," my father pointed out, but Mum wasn't listening.

To be fair to Doug, he *didn't* do it to us. He was as good as gold indoors after that, but taking him for a walk became something of a nightmare.

Our next-door neighbour bought a new car, his pride and joy. Doug showed his appreciation as well.

The lady down the street planted a hedge of little plants in front of her garden. It took her ages, partly because

she insisted on measuring the distance between their stems exactly and had to keep moving them to get it right.

The hedge was small but full of potential—until Doug discovered it. One by one, the little plants withered and died.

"I don't understand it!" wailed our neighbour.

I did.

Worst of all was when Doug targeted Mr. Brooke's white stick. Mr. Brooke can't see, but he gets around as well as anyone else by swinging his stick from side to side as he walks along. It can be painful if you pass too close. One day, I stopped to chat with Mr. Brooke, who is a piano teacher and often tells Mum it's time I started having lessons. I'd quite like to, actually, but as we stood there chatting, Doug spotted that Mr. Brooke's stick was still for once. Sadly, it was also right next to Mr. Brooke's leg—and he was wearing shorts. It's not pleasant for anyone, when Doug says hello, but it must be particularly bad for someone who doesn't know it's about to happen. I think I need say no more than that my piano lessons are now a very unlikely prospect.

I did try to get Doug to behave. I took him along to Obedience Classes. Doug excelled himself. He sat when I told him to sit. He lay down when I told him to lie down. He retrieved a stick. He walked to heel. He even rolled over and

waved his legs in the air on command. The class instructor, a hearty woman called Mrs. Blenkinsop, took me on one side.

"Paolo," she said, "I really think you are wasting your money by coming to my class. Doug is the best-behaved little dog I've ever met. In fact, I think you are putting the other class members off a little. They find it discouraging when their own animals don't live up to Doug's shining example."

"But Mrs. Blenkinsop," I began, "there really is a problem with Doug's behaviour. That's why we're here. It's..."

But just as I was about to explain, Doug did it for me.

Mrs. Blenkinsop jumped up and down and waved her arms, which sent all the other dogs in the class wild.

"Take him away! Take him away!" she shrieked.

The other owners, unable now to restrain their own pets, watched in horror as the dogs converged on Mrs. Blenkinsop's sturdy legs.

I admit it—I didn't stay to find out what happened next, but I did hear later that the class was disbanded and Mrs. Blenkinsop became allergic to dogs. That's a bit unfortunate when you make your living training them, I suppose.

Of course, I gave Doug a real talking-to after that incident, and I can say in all honesty that he never offended a dog-trainer again. But then, he never met a dog-trainer again.

After a while, I worked out a route for our daily walks that didn't take us near other people after the first bit along the pavement. It was still a lottery, of course, and I think I got a reputation for being a bit unfriendly when I was seen to cross the road when neighbours or friends approached. It was especially bad because Doug showed every sign of *wanting* to be friendly. It was just that I knew what that entailed and they didn't.

Out in the countryside, I had no fears. Doug's first attempt to make his presence felt to a cow ended in a heavy hoof making contact with his bottom, so he didn't try that again.

It's funny, isn't it, that sometimes when annoying things go on for long enough, you hardly notice them any more. After a while, it seemed normal to try to avoid people when I had Doug on

his lead. After a year or two, I really didn't think about it any more. In the family, we talked about how snooty and unfriendly all our neighbours were, completely forgetting that most of them had good reason to avoid us. In every other way, Doug was a wonderful dog.

Then, one night, Doug became even more wonderful. This is what happened.

It was summer, and the nights were as warm as the days. We slept with the windows open and sometimes forgot to close them downstairs when we went up to bed. One moonless night, it was so warm that I couldn't sleep. I tossed and turned in bed, trying not to think about a history test I had the next day. Doug, sleeping at the foot of my bed as usual, raised his head and trotted out of the door. I heard him go downstairs and supposed he wanted a drink from his water bowl.

A few minutes later, I heard a little crash, followed by another one.

"Oh Doug," I groaned, clambering out of bed. I tried to think of what he might have knocked over. It was puzzling. Mum had long ago put all our ornaments on high shelves or away in cupboards. You can't have ornaments and someone who wags his tail a lot in the same house.

I strained my ears in the darkness and heard some strange rustling sounds.

Then, quite distinctly there came the noise of the drawer of Dad's desk being slowly opened. I knew it was that because it squeaks in a peculiar way.

Now Doug is a clever dog. I would go so far as to say that he's a really exceptionally clever dog, but he hasn't yet learnt to open drawers with his teeth. I admit the hair stood up on the back of my neck as I listened.

You may wonder why Doug wasn't barking or letting us know in some other way that there was an intruder in the house. Well, it didn't really surprise me. Doug is a friendly dog. Most of the time, after all, I made sure he didn't come across any human beings. I should think he was pretty glad to *meet* another person.

I crept out of bed and tiptoed along the landing to my parents' room. They were both heavy sleepers.

"Mum! Dad!" I hissed, pulling at the covers. It took ages to wake them up. When I finally persuaded Mum to open her eyes, she screamed.

There was no time for me to explain. You couldn't miss the noise of an even louder crash downstairs and then the sound of the front door being wrenched open. Through the open window we heard footsteps running down the path. Lighter, scampering footsteps followed them. The footsteps stopped when they reached the gate. The scampering stopped.

A second later, a loud yell from the burglar told us that Doug was saying goodbye in his own sweet way.

Dad rang the police, and they arrived with surprising speed.

"We were in the neighbourhood," one of them explained. This isn't the first complaint we've had tonight. The chap is obviously working his way from house to house. We're going to round up anyone who's wandering about suspiciously in these streets and take them down to the station. Could you come down and see if you could identify one of them?

"But we didn't see him!" wailed Mum. "There's no point at all in us coming down. We don't know one single distinguishing feature about the wretched man. It could even be a woman, actually."

"We do," I said, "know a single distinguishing feature, that is." And I explained to the policeman about Doug's unfortunate habit.

The policeman grinned.

"You're sure?" he said.

"Absolutely sure," I agreed. "I've heard enough people screeching after Doug has done his dreadful deed to know what *that* sounds like. I'll be happy to bring Doug down to the station as soon as you like."

It was hardly necessary. Of the five men rounded up that night, only one had

attracted the attention of every police dog in the area. He stood, looking terrified, as one after another came along and sniffed at his trousers. Doug simply confirmed what everyone already knew—and had to be restrained from repeating his earlier actions!

"Don't let him do that!" cried a policeman. "It'll destroy the evidence!"

He gave Doug a police-dog treat as a reward for leaving the man's trousers alone—this time.

I've always said that Doug is a clever dog. That treat was enough to tell him that *not* cocking his leg at people had its rewards. He was never a dreadful dog again.

Of course, he's still pretty friendly to burglars, but you can't have everything, can you?

The Unwilling Warthog

Have you ever looked in the mirror and wished you were someone else? It happens to the best of us on a Monday morning when many of us wake up looking as if we're in dire need of a head transplant. Even supermodels, I'm told, sometimes peer into the glass and say, "Aaaaaaagh!"

Certainly, Wilbur the warthog knew all about those kinds of feelings. He didn't, of course, have a bathroom mirror, but he did have a perfectly good waterhole that reflected his ... er ... *characterful* face early each morning when he went for a drink and a wash. (Yes, it *was* in the same water, but don't let's forget he was a warthog with warthog ways.)

It didn't matter how cheerful Wilbur was feeling after a night of dreams about everything he liked best in the world. When he saw his reflection in the waterhole, he went, "Aaaaaaagh!" as if it was the first time he had ever seen his large, hairy face.

You see, Wilbur didn't want to be a warthog. I know and you know that if you are born a warthog you will be a warthog for the rest of your days, but Wilbur clung to a feeble hope that it was a mistake. He didn't mind the idea of being any other kind of animal. He just didn't like warthogs very much.

When Wilbur was still only a warthoglet, his mother found him one day mincing across the savannah and waggling his nose in the air.

"What on earth are you doing, Wilbur?" she asked. "You'll damage your trotters walking like that. Mincing is not the warthog way."

"I'm not a warthog," Wilbur replied. "I'm a rather short giraffe, but I'll grow one day soon."

Wilbur's mother called his father.

"You need to have a word with that boy," she said. "He seems to think he's a giraffe, as if anyone would want to be one of those useless, lanky lollopers. I'm glad he has ambitions, but he needs to know that there is no way he will ever be a giraffe. And thank goodness for that!"

Wilbur's father did have a word. The word was "Fathead!" and he used it liberally. Poor Wilbur looked stunned and close to tears.

"You mean I'm *never* going to be a giraffe?" he snorted plaintively. "Never ever? But surely, when I grow up..."

"When you grow up, you'll be a fine, big warthog like me," said his father, tossing his tusks proudly. "Now let's stop all this silly nonsense. Think how those giraffes would laugh at you if they knew. They're unbearably uppity as it is."

Wilbur looked in horror at his father. He saw a large animal with a tendency towards tubbiness. Wilbur's dad would have called it muscle, but it looked suspiciously like flab to the hoglet. The senior warthog's face was not, to Wilbur's mind, a thing of beauty. It was wrinkled. It was hairy. It had tusks growing out at odd angles. The eyes were small and a bit red (due to late nights at the waterhole) and the nose was large and sniffly. Wilbur, still a sweet little hoglet, showed all the signs of being a very similar warthog at a later stage in his development. He found the thought unbearable.

"You see, I don't *want* to be a warthog," he told his astonished father.

"I'd much rather be some other kind of animal. One that is graceful or fast or clever. Or all three," he added hopefully.

Wilbur's father was aghast. An aghast warthog is not a pretty sight.

"But warthogs *are* graceful," he snorted, and he trotted smartly around his son to prove his point.

Wilbur, coughing from the dust tossed up by his father's less than fairylike feet, was not impressed.

"Not as graceful as a gazelle," he said sulkily.

"Maybe not, but we are certainly fast," claimed his father. He lowered his warty nose and *charged* at an inoffensive tussock of grass in the distance. More dust

was hurled into the air as the heavy hog thundered across the savannah. A nearby antelope looked up in surprise. Warthogs were not known for their speed.

Wilbur waited until his sprinting father, badly out of breath and making a deeply unattractive sound somewhere between a snort and a wheeze, returned to his side.

"That was good," he said graciously, " but a leopard is a lot faster. And it doesn't make that strangled bagpipe noise."

Wilbur's dad took a minute or two to recover himself.

"That business about leopards being fast is over-rated in my opinion," he said. "They can't keep it up for long, while a fit warthog, perhaps a little younger than myself, can jog along for hour after hour. It's staying power that counts in the end, you know."

Now it was Wilbur's turn to snort.

"Don't say another word, Wilbur!" cried his father. "How you can even suggest that warthogs aren't clever, I don't know. Didn't your aunt Susan invent a method of waterhole wallowing that allowed maximum mud coverage? That's pretty clever, if you ask me."

"Some elephants," said Wilbur, "can remember things that happened *years* ago. Chimpanzees use sticks to dig grubs out of holes. Lionesses can creep ever so quietly though the grass until they are ready to *pounce*! Those things are really clever. And some human beings, you know, can make music come out of little boxes. Now that's what I call clever."

Wilbur's dad pawed the ground with his trotter in vexation.

"You should be proud of being a warthog, son," he said. "Imagine, you could have been born a vulture. Ugh!"

"At least I'd be able to fly," said Wilbur. "And other animals would respect me a bit."

"You call it respect. I'd call it fear and loathing," replied his father. "Surely you'd rather be a warthog than a snake? They don't even have legs!"

"They don't need them," said Wilbur. "They don't have ugly trotters and fat, hairy knees, either."

"It's no use talking to you," grunted the older warthog. "I'm going off for a good wallow."

Later, he took Wilbur's mother on one side.

"Who's been filling the boy's head with this nonsense?" he asked. "There's no finer calling in life than warthoghood. I tried to tell him that, but he wouldn't listen. He's a bit of a loner. Maybe he should spend more time with warthogs his own age. I'll ask my sister and her hoglets to visit. A bit of rough-and-tumble with his cousins will soon sort Wilbur out."

But Wilbur didn't get on at all well with five lively hoglets. He found them rough and rude. After a couple of days, the hoglets refused to even try to play with Wilbur.

"He's weird," they said. "He doesn't like mud and he snorts in a funny way. Let's go home again, Mum."

Wilbur was on his own again. His feelings of disgust at being a warthog didn't change. Mornings when he arrived at the waterhole were a nightmare to him. During his dreams, he could imagine himself a zebra or a lion. The shimmering water destroyed all such illusions. Staring back at him was (to his eyes) a perfectly hideous face, with growing tusks and little hairy ears. Wilbur tried to wash and drink with his eyes shut, but nearly drowned in the process.

Then, one day, a human being in a truck came to the waterhole. He didn't have a box that made music, but he did have a similar box that he kept holding to his face and clicking with. He made a camp near the waterhole and set about clicking at every animal he could find.

For a while, Wilbur watched the human in awe. Although not as graceful as a gazelle or as fast as a leopard, he was pretty clever. He could make a fire and drive a truck (which meant that he didn't *need* to be able to run like a leopard). He could do up buttons with his wiggly fingers, which Wilbur, looking in despair at his own stiff little trotters, envied enormously. The human being could creep, too, very like a lion, when he wanted to click at a fierce animal. He could poke grubs out of a hole with a stick just as well as a chimpanzee. At least, it wasn't exactly a hole. It was a round, shiny thing with pinkish-red grubs inside. They were obviously just as delicious as ordinary white grubs, though, because the human being ate lots of them.

Wilbur longed more than anything else to be a human being. He thought the camper was wonderful. But being a human being, he discovered, wasn't easy.

Wilbur tried sitting crosslegged, as the human did in front of his fire, and had to call for help to get his legs untangled. Wilbur tried to drive the camper's truck when he wasn't looking, and almost frightened the life out of himself when he put his trotter firmly on the horn. Finally, Wilbur tried to click with one of the human's clicking things, but although he touched it very delicately with the tips of his trotters, it made a horrible crunching sound and didn't really look the same shape afterwards. The human being made a lot of vulture-type noises and hopped up and down on the spot when he found the squashed clicker. Wilbur wondered if this marvellous creature could actually fly, but the human simply got very red in the face and had to sit down to recover. Wilbur, who had never seen a human child, wondered if perhaps the creature was still young and hadn't yet learnt to take off. He still thought the camper was the most amazing animal he had ever seen.

Wilbur's mother and father tried hard to talk him out of his adoration of the human being.

"You can't trust them," said his father. "One minute they're going, 'Oooh, aaaah! Look at the lovely animals!' The next they're trying to catch you in a net or," he added darkly, "worse."

Wilbur would hear none of it. Even when his mother told him she had heard a rumour that humans ate something called pigs, animals with snouts and trotters not unlike his own, Wilbur would not be put off. He went to sleep each night (stretched out uncomfortably in an unwarthoglike but faintly human way) wishing with all his heart that he could wake up and find that he had wiggly fingers and a tiny head.

All this time, the human had been clicking at elephants and zebras, antelopes and gazelles. He had crept through the grass to click at a lion sleeping in the sun and stood very still for hours on end until a couple of snooty giraffes deigned to drift in his direction.

Suddenly, one sunny morning, the human started clicking at warthogs.

"I don't like this," said Wilbur's father. "Come on, Mavis, we're getting out of here. Wilbur! Follow us! Ready? Quick waddle!"

But Wilbur, fascinated by his hero's activities, didn't move a muscle. And with his father, mother and various neighbours gone, he suddenly became the centre of attraction himself. The human was clicking furiously. Wilbur did his best to strike interesting poses. Somehow, they didn't make the human happy. He wanted pictures of *warthogs*, not animals that looked on the surface like warthogs but appeared to act like supermodels.

The more Wilbur posed, the more exasperated the human being appeared to become. He crept closer and closer, hoping, perhaps, to be able to click at Wilbur's face and avoid his waving trotters. Wilbur, still posing like mad, retreated to the muddiest part of the waterhole. The human advanced.

Now Wilbur could have told the human being quite a lot about how to negotiate the terribly muddy mud at the edge of the waterhole, but he was too busy posing even to snort in alarm. There was a sudden cry of, "*Ooooooooeeerr*!" and a enormouis *SPLASH*! Suddenly the waterhole was full of a wallowing warthog, a spluttering human and a couple of curious crocodiles, who had slithered off the bank to see what all the fuss was about.

Wilbur wondered the same thing. The human being was making an incredible amount of noise and splashing, splattering Wilbur and the crocodiles with mud and water in a way they rather enjoyed.

It was a while before Wilbur realized that the human was in distress. It was several moments longer before his brain could take in the awful truth—this human could not swim!

A warthog's mind does not work particularly quickly. By the time Wilbur decided he must take some action, the human had managed to find some mud under his feet and begin to stagger to the edge of the waterhole. It was then that he saw the crocodiles...

Now Wilbur had the sense to know that a young and frisky crocodile can be less than friendly, but to be afraid of old Gladys and Fred seemed ridiculous. All of a sudden, Wilbur saw the human with new eyes. He simply looked silly.

I won't say that Wilbur became proud of his warthogishness overnight, but from that day he did see himself in a different light. It wasn't long before he found he could think of something to despise about every creature—not just humans. And this, although not a very pleasant characteristic, is typical of warthogs the world over. At last, Wilbur was an unwilling warthog no longer.

Carol and the Contest Car

Each morning when she woke up, Carol looked out of the window to make sure her car was still there. It's the kind of thing a lot of people do, especially in areas where things have to be chained down to stay in one place for more than an hour or two, but it's not so usual for someone of Carol's age to *have* a car. She was eight years and two months old. And it really was her car. She had won it in a competition at the supermarket.

It was a bright Saturday morning when Carol and her mother went shopping. The supermarket was packed, as usual.

"This is hopeless," said Carol's mum, looking at the queues. "Let's go and raid the café."

Although the rest of the shop was heaving with people, the café was usually very quiet. That was because the coffee was disgusting and the sandwiches looked as if they had died in the night. But Carol and her mother weren't worried about coffee or sandwiches. For some reason, the café served the best chocolate cake either of them had ever tasted. They ate it with lemonade and it was a real treat. So far, only a few other people seemed to have discovered it.

The lady behind the counter greeted Carol and her mother like old friends.

"The usual?" she asked, but she didn't even wait for a reply. She was already cutting big wedges of cake and dumping it unceremoniously on to thick white plates.

Carol and her mother didn't mind that the cake looked as though it had been through a mincer before they even tasted it. It was, after all, the taste that was heavenly.

"Mmmmmmm," said Carol.

"Mmm mmm *mmmm*," replied her mother. "This is what makes shopping bearable. Mmmm."

The lady from behind the counter was passing their table, wiping up crumbs from other tables in a way that only made them look worse. She laughed when she heard what Mrs. Ferguson was saying.

"It wouldn't be half as bad, dear, if you won that car," she said. "It's trudging home with the shopping that takes it out of you, in my opinion."

Mrs. Ferguson privately thought that the whole experience (except the cake) took it out of her, but she asked, "What car?" all the same.

"Oh, there's a lovely new car to be won in aisle five," said the lady. "All you have to do is to guess how many cornflakes there are in a box."

"Couldn't you just buy some and see how many were usually in the box?" asked Carol's mother.

"Oh no, dear!" laughed the woman. "It's a huge box. It's bigger than your little one here. That's why it's hard. Mind you, there have been students from the university here all week taking all sorts of measurements and doing calculations on their computers. They reckon they can work it out what they call scientifically."

"Hmmm, it doesn't sound as if we stand much of a chance then," said Mrs. Ferguson, eating the last crumbs of her chocolate cake.

"It's still worth a go, though," said the café lady. "You only have to buy one box of cornflakes to try. And after all, you'd probably be doing that anyway."

"Mum," said Carol, as they brushed the chocolate crumbs from their laps and went back to the entrance to find a trolley, "you won't do anything *silly*, will you?"

Mrs. Ferguson snorted.

"Whatever give you that idea?" she demanded. "Silly, indeed!"

Carol mentioned gherkins, sardines and toothpaste, of which the household still had big enough supplies to last until they were all in their nineties, including Carol.

"That was different," said her mother. "There was a real chance of winning with those competitions, and why we didn't, I can't imagine. I'm sure

all these contests are rigged, you know. I've got absolutely no intention of buying cornflakes we don't want and don't need in order to enter a competition we don't stand a chance of winning."

But when the pair, steering their trolley at dangerous speed along the aisles, suddenly came around the corner into aisle five and saw the car, they stopped dead in their tracks.

"Oh," said Carol's mother.

"Ah," said Carol.

There was something about that car. It gleamed under the shop lights. Its slinky headlights shone and its windows twinkled. It was a shiny silver colour, with a red stripe down the side. Silver and red were Carol's favourite colours. And best of all was its number plate: CF1.

Carol looked at her mother. Her mother looked back.

"How many boxes of cornflakes could we eat in a year?" asked Carol.

"Loads," said her mother, and began to pull some off the shelf. The trolley was soon full.

"We've got sixty-four boxes," Mrs. Ferguson told the assistant standing near an enormous box of cornflakes. "Where do I make my guesses?"

Mrs. Ferguson sat down at the table provided with a sheaf of entry forms. It took her ages and ages to fill them all in.

"Four million, seven hundred thousand and three," she wrote on the first form. "Nine hundred and forty-eight thousand and seventy- two," she wrote on the second. Carol sighed. It was clear that her mother had not the faintest idea how many cornflakes could possibly be in the box. The likelihood of her winning seemed very small indeed.

After what seemed like ages, Mrs. Ferguson stopped writing and shook her wrists vigorously.

"It makes your arm ache, writing so fast," she said. "It reminds me of exams at school. Well, we've done our best. Now we just have to wait."

She got up to leave with the huge trolleyful of boxes, but the assistant called her back and pointed to the floor under the table.

"You dropped one," she said. "You might as well have all your goes."

"Oh, I couldn't write another one," said Mrs. Ferguson. "You do it, Carol."

Carol screwed up her eyes. Then she wrote down the biggest number she could possibly think of. Then she added three noughts for luck, put down her name and address, and helped her mother struggle home with the shopping. It involved ... er

... *borrowing* the trolley (and to be honest there were already three of those in the back garden from the gherkin, sardine and toothpaste fiascos).

I wish I could say that both Carol and her mother forgot all about the contest in the weeks that followed, but it's hard to forget about cornflakes when your bedroom is piled high with boxes of them and you are eating them for breakfast, lunch and supper.

After a week and a half, Carol hoped she would never see another cornflake in her life. When Christmas came and went, and most of their relatives had been less than enthusiastic about receiving a breakfast product as a present, the pile hardly seemed to have lessened at all. Mrs. Ferguson wondered idly if she could build a conservatory with the boxes. Carol remembered an ill-fated attempt to make modern sculpture with sardine cans and begged her not to try.

It was one day in early February when a letter arrived addressed to Ms. C. Ferguson. Carol's mother opened it, read it and collapsed under the table.

When Carol had revived her by flapping a magazine in her face and sprinkling water over her (well, sloshing would be a more accurate term), Mrs.

Ferguson sat up and reached for the letter. She read it again and gulped.

"I won the car!" she said. "The cornflake car—I won it! No more trudging for us. It'll be wizzing all the way! I can't believe it!"

Carol looked at the letter.

"You shouldn't," she said, "it's not true. Look!"

"I have looked," replied her mother. "I've looked three times. It's perfectly clear. It's on proper headed paper. It's not a hoax or one of our relatives trying to pay us back for the cornflake presents. This is the genuine article. Look, there's a phone number to use. I'm going to ring up and confirm it."

Before Carol could say another word, her mother was on the phone and arranging for delivery. Carol bit her lip. She couldn't decide whether to say anything or not. It seemed a terrible shame to disappoint her mother, who was now dancing some kind of cancan around the kitchen and unfortunately bringing quite a few sardine cans, stashed in odd places, hurtling around her head.

Carol went up to her bedroom and consulted her ancient teddy bear.

"The thing is," she said, "I know it was my ticket that won. I know the

number off by heart and it's on the letter. But Mum hasn't been as happy as this for years. And I can't even drive for another nine years. Should I tell her or not?"

The old bear looked glum.

"I knew you'd say that," said Carol. "Okay, I'll keep quiet."

Carol crept around for the rest of the day, weighed down by her guilty secret. Her mother was on the phone to various of her friends who, over the years, had made cutting remarks about the insane waste of money that entering competitions represented. Mrs. Ferguson was obviously enjoying herself hugely.

The man from the cornflake company arrived bright and early the next morning. He tried to persuade Mrs. Ferguson to allow him to take her picture with the car, but Carol's mother, who had been spreading the word all afternoon and evening the day before, suddenly became coy and refused. As a matter of fact, this was because she hadn't been to the hairdresser for a few weeks and didn't want to appear at less than her best.

"Well," said the cornflake man at last, when he had given up trying to persuade her, "I'll leave you to enjoy your new car. If you can just give me the entry form ticket, I'll be on my way. You did keep it, didn't you?"

"Oh yes, no problem," said Mrs. Ferguson. "I stuck them on the fridge with all my other important papers. Now let me see."

There were sixty-three tickets stuck on to the fridge with magnets in the shape of sardines (consolation prizes in the sardine competition). It took some time for Mrs. Ferguson to work through them all. At last she gave a sigh of satisfaction.

"Here you are," she said. "D798324. That's it."

The man shook his head.

"No, I need D798325," he said.

Mrs. Ferguson began frantically to fan through her tickets again, but Sarah, clutching her old bear for moral support, decided it was time to speak up.

"Here it is," she said. "D798325. It's my ticket."

There was an awful silence in the kitchen as Carol's mother gazed at her with a glazed expression.

"But *I'm* Ms. C. Ferguson," she said plaintively.

"So am I," said Carol. "And it is my ticket. There isn't anything to stop me winning the car, is there?"

"No," said the cornflake man, glad now that he hadn't bothered to take lots of photos of Carol's mother. "I can't persuade you to pose for publicity shots, I suppose?" he added.

"No," said Carol. "I'd just like the keys, please."

By the time the man had left, Mrs. Ferguson had recovered a little.

"Well," she said, "I don't suppose it matters very much which one of us has won it. Shall we go for a drive right now? Aren't we lucky?"

But Carol had begun to see possibilities in her car.

"I don't think we need to go anywhere in it today," she said. "I'll think about when we can use it."

Mrs. Ferguson narrowed her eyes.

"I can see the way your mind is working and I don't like it, my girl," she said. "What's to stop me just grabbing the keys and doing what I like?"

"I'll swallow them," said Carol.

"You couldn't! Don't be ridiculous. They're much too big," scoffed her mother, but when Carol opened her mouth wide and dangled the keys over it, she squealed, "No, don't! You'll choke or something!"

"I need to go upstairs and talk to old bear," said Carol, "before I decide what to do."

Mrs. Ferguson knew when she was beaten. She gnashed her teeth and paced up and down while Carol took her time deciding on her strategy.

Carol came downstairs at last. She was carrying a list.

1. No more cornflakes - ever.
2. No more gherkins - ditto.
3. Need I mention sardines?
4. No speeding.
5. No racing.
6. No eating crisps in the car.

Mrs. Ferguson clenched her teeth, stomped up and down a bit—and agreed.

"Sometimes, Carol," she said, "I wonder which of us is the grown-up."

"Or which of us isn't," said Carol.

Princess Pearl

When King Brian and Queen Madge gave birth to their first child, the whole country held its breath for news. All night long, there was to-ing and fro-ing at the palace. Down the echoing corridors, messages from Dr. Bartfinkle, the famous physician, were relayed from one footman to another.

"More hot water!" came the cry.

"More hot water! More hot water! More hot water!" repeated the footmen in their red uniforms.

As the night wore on, the requests became stranger.

"More magazines!"

"More footballs!"

"More knicker elastic!"

"More cheese!"

There was, in fact, a perfectly good explanation for all these requests, but it doesn't have anything to do with this

story. The next important event as far as the new baby was concerned was a loud yell from the royal bedroom.

"Aaaaaagh!" shouted the Queen in an unqueenly way.

"Aaaaaagh!" shouted the new baby in a babylike way.

"Aaaaaagh!" shouted the first footman in a ridiculous way.

"Aaaaaagh!"

"Aaaaaagh!"

"Aaaaaagh!"

"Aaaaaagh!"

The cry echoed through the palace, until it reached the cook in the palace kitchens. And she, being a wise woman and well able to interpret the oddest orders, burst into tears and said, "It's a princess! God bless her!"

The usual practice, when a royal baby was born, was for the proud father to appear on the balcony in front of the palace and show the precious infant to the gathering crowds below. They, I'm afraid, having been celebrating the birth already for several hours, sometimes shouted out things that were not fit for any royal child's ears. It was often a blushing and anxious king or prince who scuttled back inside with his beautiful bundle.

On this occasion, however, no such appearance was made. Indeed, the door of the Queen's chamber remained shut for days. A thoughtful-looking Dr. Bartfinkle finally emerged, shaking his head.

The crowd waiting outside the palace included several eager newspaper reporters. They surged forward as soon as they saw the shiny black hat of the world-famous doctor.

"Is the baby well, Doctor?" they yelled. "There have been rumours that she is ill in some way."

The doctor shook his head.

"The royal princess is perfectly healthy in every way," he said. "There is nothing to worry about *there*."

The way he said these words strongly implied that there *was* something to worry about somewhere else. Like bloodhounds on the scent, the reporters were determined to find it.

"The Queen? Is she recovering well? Was it a difficult birth?"

"All births require a great deal of skill from a specialist physician," replied Dr. Bartfinkle solemnly (if untruthfully), "but I am happy to say that the Queen is doing very well and was up and about remarkably quickly."

There was a puzzled buzzing from the press pack. Then one of them asked the question they had all been wondering about since the birth.

"Why haven't we seen the baby?"

The doctor paused. His usually suave demeanor left him. His famous hat tilted over one eye. His famous frown intensified. Sweat broke out on his brow.

"I really couldn't say," he said. "No doubt the palace will keep you informed."

He scuttled into his carriage and rattled away, fanning himself with his gloves and shaking his head.

For the next few days, wild rumours and extraordinary speculations swept the kingdom. Some said that the child had been stolen just after birth and was being held to ransom. Others claimed that the Queen's maid had dropped the infant and given her a black eye, with which she could not appear in public. Old people who still believed in magic were sure that the princess had been bewitched.

None of them was right.

Back in the palace, the King had called in his most trusted advisors and sworn them to secrecy. He needed advice and he needed it badly. Finally, after seven long days of council meetings, a royal edict was sent out. All looking glasses in the kingdom were to be destroyed. It had been proved, said the edict, that looking at one's own reflection could have a dreadful effect on one's wellbeing.

Now, like me, no doubt you have had mornings when the sight of your face in the bathroom mirror was enough to send you screaming into a darkened room. But most days, the familiar features that grin back at you from the glass are not so bad. Sometimes they even look pretty good. A sensible person knows that there are good mirrors and bad mirrors, and avoids the latter at all costs. So there was a lot of muttering when the royal edict was made known.

The muttering did not die down. In the end, the famous Dr. Bartfinkle was forced to issue a learned book in which he discussed all the many ways in which poor, unsuspecting people were doing themselves untold damage by looking at their own reflections.

The doctor's reputation meant that at least half the population now took the edict seriously. The other half took the King's Army seriously. This band of military misfits was entrusted with the job of removing all looking glasses from the realm. Since the King's Army was one of

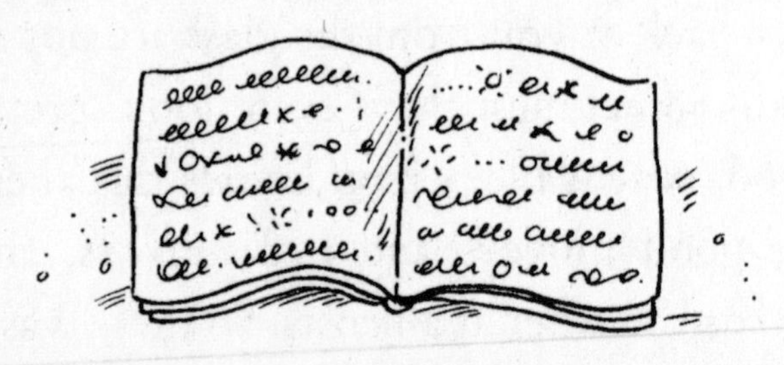

the main reasons the country could boast a very small prison population, most people thought it better not to argue when burly soldiers knocked on their doors. Within a fortnight, all the mirrors in the country had been destroyed.

This simple act had devastating results throughout the kingdom. The sales of lipsticks and eyeliners plummeted. No one wants to appear in public with a mouth spreading from ear to ear or eyes that look as if they belong to a panda. For a brief period, sales of shiny saucepans trebled, until the palace got wise to this and ordered that in future all saucepans and other shiny items must be painted black inside and out.

You have probably guessed by now what was the problem with young Princess Pearl, as she was called. She was ugly—not just ugly in the red and wriggly way that lots of babies are ugly, but ugly in a way that made footmen make faces (which they are trained not to do).

Of course, the King and Queen realized that their daughter was not the picture of perfection they had expected. I mean, all princesses are pretty, aren't they? But they loved their daughter dearly and wanted her life to be as pleasant as possible for her.

"She may grow out of it," said the King, hopefully.

"With that nose?" asked the Queen, not so hopefully.

"Something could surely be done about her eyebrows?" ventured the King.

"But not her eyes," replied his wife. Having spent her life trying to look like every subject's idea of what a queen should be, the Queen knew all too well what miracles make-up and a loyal royal beautician could achieve—and what they could not.

Meanwhile, Princess Pearl grew up to enjoy all the things that princesses usually like. She loved to ride her pony in the park. She liked to swish up and down the corridors in her best silk dresses. She liked to try on her crown. But she didn't grow any prettier.

She wasn't, of course, kept locked up in the palace from the day she was born. The King's subjects soon became all too aware of the Princess's problem, but they were far too loyal to say anything about it in print or to her face.

The most important thing as far as the King and Queen were concerned was that Princess Pearl should not herself know how extraordinarily ugly she was.

"It would destroy her confidence," said the Queen. "That's why the edict about the mirrors was so important. We really cannot have a future queen of this country who hides in her room all day. And that, you mark my words, is what would happen if she ever found out."

As time went by, the likelihood that Pearl would one day become Queen became greater, for the royal couple had no more children. As the Princess approached her eighteenth birthday, the Queen for the first time raised a subject that had been on her mind for years.

"What," she said to the King as they enjoyed a royal picnic one day, "are we going to do about finding her a husband?"

The King's answering sigh showed that his wife was not the only one who had considered this matter over the years. It was a ghastly question.

"Are there any princes with ... er ... poor eyesight?" queried the King.

"What a ridiculous idea!" cried the Queen, but she later admitted that there were not—she had checked.

"Perhaps if we offered some presents—a couple of castles, perhaps, or a lake or two?" suggested the King.

"Our daughter deserves better than that," the Queen replied sharply. "She may not be pretty, but she's a dear, sweet girl. We can't possibly marry her off to some mercenary prince who's only interested in adding another castle to his collection."

"You're right," agreed the King, looking a little ashamed, "it's just that..."

"I know," said the Queen. "Believe, me, I know."

"If she doesn't marry," groaned the King, "you know what it will mean."

The royal couple stared glumly at the distant mountains.

"It will mean Melvin," they said in chorus. "Ugh!"

The Prince Melvin in question was a very distant cousin of the King. He was a particularly objectionable man. After his last visit, before Princess Pearl's birth, when he had offended everyone, caused the footmen to go on strike, asked if he might have fried lizards for breakfast and stalked the royal cat with a toasting fork,

the royal family had decided never to invite him again. He was, however, their nearest living relative, and if Princess Pearl died without having children, he would be the next king.

"It wouldn't be *him*, of course," said the Queen, trying to look on the bright side. "He's our age. It would be one of his children."

"Darling, do you imagine that any of his children, if they take after him and his equally objectionable wife, will be any better?" asked the King. "The whole idea makes me quake in my boots, but I admit that it is very likely to happen. However, we mustn't give up without trying. We should hold a party as is customary for Pearl on her birthday and ... here's a thought ... what if it was a *masked* ball?"

"That's brilliant!" cried the Queen. "At least, it's worth a try."

Preparations for Princess Pearl's Birthday Ball were soon in full swing. Invitations were sent to every eligible prince for hundreds of miles. After some thought, the King and Queen extended the guest-list to quite a lot of eligible dukes, earls and lords as well.

For weeks, the royal cooks planned and baked, the royal gardeners pruned and clipped, the royal maids polished and plumped, and the royal footmen ran up and down the corridors shouting. At last

the ballroom was festooned with flowers, a cake of monstrous proportions was prepared, and Princess Pearl put on her gold and silver dress and the larger-than-usual (because of the nose!) mask that had been made for her by the royal jewellers. As the guests trooped in, the band struck up and the thousand twinkling lights of the chandeliers made a fairytale world.

It was a glorious party. What pleased the King and Queen more than anything was that one young man in particular spent a great deal of time dancing with the Princess and even longer talking with her on the balcony. They seemed to be getting on very well.

"Who is he?" hissed the King to the Queen, as they passed each other in a royal rumba.

"Not a clue!" mouthed the Queen, performing a tricky twizzle.

Later, as midnight drew near, the King and Queen seized the opportunity for a quick consultation.

"The trouble is," said the King, "at midnight, all masks will be removed. What will he do then?"

"As long as he behaves like a gentleman and doesn't faint, scream or throw a tantrum, I shall be happy," said the Queen.

Still, as the clock struck, she held her breath, forgetting even to remove her own mask (which didn't really matter as the royal crown was rather a give-away). All eyes were on the Princess and her partner as they removed their masks.

As the Princess revealed her face at last, there was quite a bit of fainting, screaming and throwing of tantrums in the room, but it didn't come from the young man gazing deeply into Pearl's eyes. It was obvious even to the Princess's worried father that the unknown suitor was already far too much in love to be seeing straight at all.

"Love," said the Queen with feeling, echoing his own thoughts, "is a wonderful thing."

Suddenly, the young man hurried from the room and returned carrying a present wrapped in pink and silver paper with a large pink bow.

"Happy birthday, darling," he said.

While the King went red and made a sort of "Hrrrrrummmpph" sound at what he considered was undue familiarity from someone whose name he didn't even know, Princess Pearl was unwrapping her present with eagerness.

It was a beautiful, jewelled … mirror!

The Queen started forward, then froze. The King turned from white to red, then back to white. Everyone else in the room held their breaths. There was an awesome silence as the Princess turned over the mirror. She looked. She made a little face. She glanced up at the young man. "Does it matter?" she asked.

"What?" asked the suitor, gazing at her like a puppy.

"I didn't think so," said the Princess. And—to the consternation of the King—she kissed her young man right there in the ballroom.

There was a storm of clapping from the assembled party. The Queen sighed and burst into tears. The King strode forward to find out who exactly he was about to have as a future son-in-law.

"May I have the honour to present myself, Your Highness," said the young man, bowing satisfactorily low, "as Prince James, son of Prince Melvin, your distant cousin, and, if I may be so bold, a suitor for your daughter's hand."

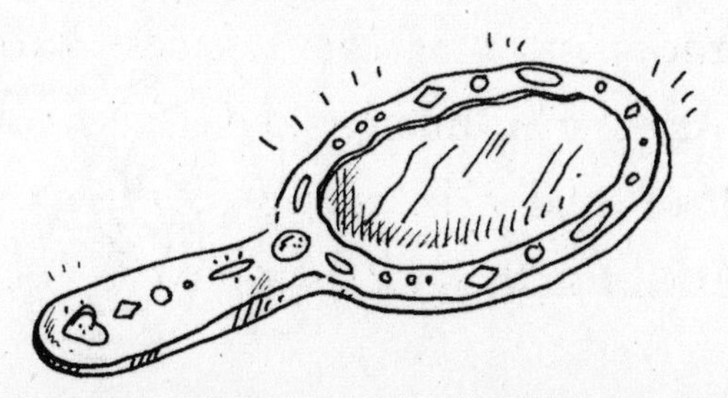

It was almost unbelievable that the objectionable Melvin could have so fine a son. Prince James was tactful, but the royal couple gathered that being brought up by such an unpleasant man had made the Prince value the inside of a person far beyond their outer appearance. He was a perfect match for Princess Pearl.

As for Pearl herself, many people wondered why she had not screamed at the very first sight of herself. What they had not considered is that when you look deeply into another person's eyes, what you see is … yourself. Pearl had already had several long minutes to view her formidable features in the Prince's eyes and to decide that if liked them, then she could too.

As the Queen said, love really is a wonderful thing.

A House in a Huff

People sometimes talk about houses having an atmosphere.

"The place felt friendly the first time we set foot in it," you hear them say.

"There's something unpleasant about this place. It's spooky," someone else may comment—about exactly the same house. Yes, people have strong opinions about how a place *feels.*

But have you ever wondered how the *house* feels? If you think for one moment that houses don't have feelings, you're wrong. It's just that they don't usually show them. But think about it. Haven't you ever walked past a really snooty terrace? Or looked out of the window at a smiling thatched cottage?

The house in this story was a perfectly ordinary family house. It was built about a hundred years ago and had four bedrooms, a living room, a study, a

large kitchen and a conservatory at the back. There was also a bathroom upstairs and a cloakroom downstairs.

For most of its hundred years, the house stood quietly enough, putting up with whatever happened to it. It didn't complain when someone took out all the fireplaces and put radiators in. It didn't get upset when the front door was painted purple and orange sometime around 1965. About thirty years later, when the new occupants put back all the fireplaces that had been taken out before, it simply sighed and got on with being a house. It wasn't until the Barker family arrived that the house began to fight back.

The Barkers were a large family, with a mother, a father, a grandmother and six children. It was a squeeze to fit them into four bedrooms, so the family decided to make two more rooms in the attics. That would have been fine (the house quite liked the idea of windows in the roof) but unfortunately Mr. Barker, always keen to save money, decided to do the work himself.

Mr. Barker was enthusiastic and hardworking. He was also clumsy, impetuous and unwilling to listen to advice of any kind. He was exactly the kind of person you do *not* want fiddling with your joists or tinkering with your tiles. From the moment he first put his head up through the trapdoor and said the immortal words, “Oh yes, nothing to it!”, the die was cast.

In the first week of operations, Mr. Barker backed into the cold-water tank while holding an electric drill. Several hundred gallons of water later (mainly in the kitchen, but passing through two bedrooms and the bathroom on their way and taking the floors with them), Mr. Barker could be heard vigorously swishing with a mop and complaining about the standard of workmanship in old houses.

It took five months for the damage to be repaired. Mr. Barker tried to do it himself, but after the second time that his mother had fallen through the newly installed bathroom floor in nothing but her dentures, he decided to call in a friend to help. The friend, who at least had some inkling of the size of the job involved, called in a building firm. The building firm, aware that it was hardly safe to *be* in the house, let alone work on it, ordered everybody out and got to work.

Naturally, Mr. Barker, already smarting at the cost of the building work, was not keen to pay for a hotel or even to rent another home for his large family. Three large tents were erected in the garden. The water butt became an improvised bathtub—although it feels a bit odd to bath standing up.

There followed the coldest three months the area had ever known. Mr. Barker tried to cheer up his shivering family by building a large bonfire in the middle of the garden. He threw on to it all the wood that the builders were tearing out of the house, but unfortunately included quite a lot of the wood that they were trying to put back *in* again. Piles of varnished floorboards made the fire a little *too* successful. Sparks went into the kitchen, and only the fact that it had never dried out completely from the flood saved it from being destroyed completely. As it was, the builders still had to replace the new ceiling they had only just installed.

After six days in the tents, several of the family's neighbours took pity on them. Each of them took in one member of the family, and although it was hard to find anyone to take Mr. Barker himself (his offer to do odd jobs for his host may have had something to do with it), they were all accommodated at last.

The children found that living in another person's home brought with it mixed advantages. Although Tommy loved the toffees dished out by Mrs. Washburton, he couldn't stand her three Persian cats. Angela enjoyed the food at the Thatchers' but hated the way she had to do *all* the washing up. Mrs. Barker had a particularly hard time with Mr. Evans, who, having inveigled a woman into his house at last, saw no reason why he should ever have to do cleaning, ironing or cooking again. On the other hand, it was much better than freezing to death in the garden, and, to be fair, it wasn't only the Barkers who suffered. Mrs. Merton, who took in Mr. Barker, never quite managed to control her central heating again, after her lodger had overhauled it for her.

You will hardly believe it, I know, but the day the Barkers moved back into their newly repaired house was the day that Mr. Barker made another start on the attic conversion. He had, he told his wife, done a lot of thinking about the best way to approach the task (and it wasn't moving backwards with an electric drill in his hand). Although Mrs. Barker had deep misgivings, she tried not to think about what might be happening above her head as she moved about the house.

This time, Mr. Barker decided to begin by installing the windows in the roof. Of course, this involved removing tiles. Naturally, the biggest storm for fifty years chose that moment to strike.

"You'd be amazed how much water these old tiles let through," Mr. Barker told his wife, as the first drops began to fall from the sky.

"Especially," said Mrs. Barker, "when they're not *there*!"

This time, it was the upper rooms and the sitting room (yes, the ceiling came down, having escaped last time) that suffered. Once again, the friend was called in. Once again, the builders followed. Once again, the neighbours gritted their teeth to help out the Barkers.

This time the repairs only took three months. It was long enough. By the time the family moved back into the

house, they had spent more time *not* living in it than sleeping under its roof. At least it now *had* a roof!

Mr. Barker spent over two weeks redecorating. He attempted to mix his own paint from leftovers and was halfway through painting the sitting room a kind of sludge colour when Mrs. Barker came home and put her foot down.

Unfortunately, she put it down in the baking tray that Mr. Barker had pressed into service to hold the paint. Sludge-coloured paint flew everywhere, giving a sort of camouflaged air to the whole room. Mr. Barker, declaring that he liked the effect, was ready to live with it, but Mrs. Barker (hopping, not putting her foot down) sent him straight out to buy white paint and a proper paint-tray.

The white paint (selling at a suspiciously cheap price in the local DIY store and seized upon by Mr. Barker for that reason) took thirteen coats to cover the sludge. Mr. Barker was exhausted when he had finished.

But did that stop him turning his attention, one more time, to the attic? It did not! On Saturday morning, at the breakfast table, Mr. Barker told the whole family that it was time he got started on the attic again.

Mrs. Barker, deciding that the time for a dramatic gesture had come, actually got on her knees to beg him to call in the builders. Mr. Barker's mother, although eighty-two and having complained about the state of her knees every day for the last fifteen years, joined her daughter-in-law on the quarry tiles.

Mr. Barker, I'm sorry to say, laughed. His faith in his own abilities was so great that he could not believe anyone would seriously suggest he wasn't up to the job. Despite all the evidence to the contrary, Mr. Barker thought he was almost a genius where DIY was concerned. Of course, when you're working on an old house, there can be problems…

Mr. Barker left his mother and wife grovelling and went cheerily upstairs to the attic. This time, he thought he would start with the floor.

BREAD

It was at the moment when Mr. Barker, hammer in hand, approached the electrical cables running along the attic (slightly in the wrong place, he thought) that the house, at long last, decided to intervene. It simply could not stand the idea of more builders, more bashing and more bungling. With a little shrug of what would have been its shoulders if they hadn't been rafters, the house upended Mr. Barker, who landed heavily on his bottom and a box of tin tacks.

When, despite this heavy hint, Mr. Barker, not without some regrettable language, staggered to his feet, the house took action again. A flipped floor plank was all it took to send Mr. Barker flying unceremoniously through the trapdoor. He bounced on the landing but failed to stop, sliding with a loud *bump! bump! bumpity bump!* down the stairs to arrive in a heap in the front hall.

When the two Mrs. Barkers rushed to his aid, the DIY expert was moaning on the floor—and certainly not laughing very much any more.

Mr. Barker was in bed with a fractured ankle and bruised ribs for a week. After that he started to totter about on his crutches. When he was down to one crutch only, the foolish man picked up a screwdriver and started checking electrical switches. He was not in the least

concerned by the fact that he knew *nothing* about switches. Before long, one or two of them were smouldering quietly, and it was only young Tommy coming home and sniffing suspiciously that alerted the family to the impending fire.

Next morning, no one was at home except the hobbling handyman. Did Mr. Barker sit quietly in a chair and read a nice book? Did he flop on the couch in front of the TV? Did he sit in the garden and wonder what to do about the burnt patch that even weeds wouldn't grow on? No. He picked up a spanner and set off to try to sort out a strange noise he had detected in the cloakroom's plumbing.

The house had had enough. It was determined that not another drop of water would stain its woodwork. Afterwards, Mr. Barker was never quite sure how it happened. It is enough to say that when the family arrived home that afternoon, there definitely were some strange sounds coming from the cloakroom's plumbing. Mr. Barker was head down in the toilet, making sounds of distress.

You might think that such a rush of blood to the head would have a sobering effect on the DIY-er. On the contrary. All it meant was that Mr. Barker felt unwilling to do more work inside the house. Instead, he went outside with a hammer and cast meaningful glances at the conservatory.

"What are you thinking of doing?" asked Mrs. Barker with great trepidation.

"This conservatory has never been big enough," said her husband. "I'm thinking of taking it down and building a larger one. If I make a really big one, it will even cover this burnt patch on the grass. It'll kill two birds with one stone."

Mrs. Barker was saved by the bell. One of her husband's friends chose that moment to arrive and find out how the invalid was doing. With a sigh of relief, the poor woman went back inside, hopeful that the next time her husband found himself with a hammer in his hand, he would have forgotten all about the conservatory.

If only he had. The next time he was alone in the house, Mr. Barker, who no longer needed his crutches, put on his protective gloves and goggles and picked up his heaviest mallet. He approached the conservatory with rising glee ... he did not appear to be getting any closer to it!

Yes, the house, taking the only course it could now think of, was edging away from its tormenter. Inch by inch it shuffled towards the road, with Mr. Barker, his mouth open in astonishment, following. When it reached the gate (which it flattened), the house got up on

its toes and picked up its speed. It was positively trotting as it hurried down the hill. By the time it had gone over the crossroads, the house had got into its stride. It was too fast for Mr. Barker to catch, especially with an ankle only recently out of plaster.

Mrs. Barker returned home later that day to a scene that even in her worst nightmares she had never considered. A small crowd was standing outside her gate. Nothing very much at all was standing inside it. Only Mr. Barker was sitting on the ground, surrounded by manholes, foundations, and a lot of bare earth and spiders.

"What have you done to the house!" wailed Mrs. Barker.

"I'm not sure," replied her husband, "but I've been thinking that it would be better to start again from scratch anyway.

So it's all for the best. These old places often are not worth repairing, you know. By the time you've finished, you would have been better to build a whole new house. I thought that was what we'd do. Or rather, I think I could tackle it myself, if I got a book from the library."

Mrs. Barker would have packed her bags, but her bags were in the house, wherever *that* was. What on earth was she going to tell the children?

Just then, a farmer on a tractor rumbled up the road. When he saw the crowd and the empty plot, he paused.

"Are you missing a house?" he enquired, turning off his engine. "We've got a strange one down in the lower paddock. It looks good there, but it doesn't belong to us so I don't feel quite comfortable about it. Can you come and talk it back home again?"

Mrs. Barker thought she could. She climbed on to the back of the tractor and set off for her huffy home. Late that night, a rather shamefaced house and a triumphant Mrs. Barker arrived back in the garden.

Everything was back to normal, but the strange thing was that somewhere on the journey home every single tool that Mr. Barker ever possessed got mysteriously lost. For years afterwards, local anglers achieved extraordinary catches in the river at the bottom of the hill.

Bryony and her Brothers

Bryony was an only child. When she first asked her parents if she could have a brother, her mother laughed and said, "Well, we'll see what we can do about it."

Bryony waited for what seemed like years. It was two and a half days.

"Is he coming today?" she asked her mother. "My brother, I mean."

Mrs. Beales explained that having babies took a long time. Much, much longer than two and a half days.

"It's almost as long as from one birthday to the next," she told her little girl. "You just have to be patient."

Bryony was patient. She didn't even mention the matter for a least a month. Then her best friend Rosa told her she had a secret to tell.

"Secrets aren't meant to be told," said Bryony. But Rosa was bursting with the news and couldn't wait to let her friend know that she was going to have a baby sister in the summer.

All Bryony's old longings came flooding back. She went to play at Rosa's house and noticed that Rosa's mum was looking fat.

"It's the baby!" laughed Mrs. Branson, when Bryony prodded her tummy with a toy trumpet.

That night, Bryony looked critically at her mother and said, "You're too thin!"

"It's the first time anyone has ever said *that* to me!" laughed Mrs. Beales. "What makes you think so, Bry?"

Bryony told her mother about Mrs. Branson and the new baby. Bryony's mother looked a little sad.

"Sometimes babies don't just come along when you want them, Bry," she said. "You'll have to wait a little bit longer."

There didn't seem to be any choice. Bryony didn't want to leave it to chance that her parents would forget about this important matter, though. On her Christmas list, she asked Santa for skates, a doll's house and a brother. The doll's house and the skates came along perfectly, but Santa seemed not to have noticed the other item.

On her birthday list Bryony put:

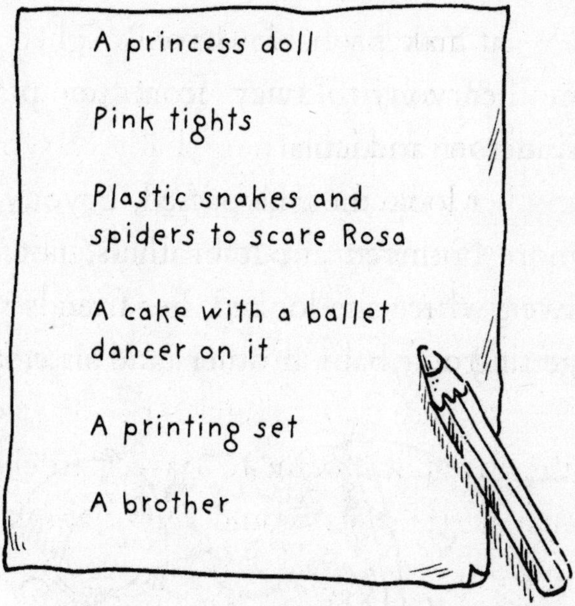

A princess doll

Pink tights

Plastic snakes and spiders to scare Rosa

A cake with a ballet dancer on it

A printing set

A brother

The princess doll, the pink tights, the cake with the ballet dancer and the printing set all arrived on schedule. The plastic snakes and spiders didn't, but Bryony bought them anyway after saving up her pocket money.

"I was saving it up to buy something for my new brother," she told her mother, "but I've probably got time to save up again before then."

"You probably have," sighed her mother, edging away from the plastic spiders in particular.

As the months passed, Bryony got more bothered about brothers, not less. Everywhere she looked, her friends were getting new baby brothers and sisters.

"It's not all fun, you know," Rosa tried to comfort her. "They shout a lot and

Mum and Dad don't have much time for me at the moment. But I think it'll be worth it when she's big enough to play with. And she has the cutest little clothes, look! Aren't these socks sweet?"

Bryony decided that another talk with her parents was necessary. She found her mother working at the computer.

"I need to talk to you about my brother," she said. "I'm just worried that I'll be too old by the time he gets here."

"You and me both," replied her mother with feeling. "But you know, Bryony, sometimes we just can't have everything we want *when* we want it. Daddy and I would like to have another baby too. We've even been to see if the doctor can help. I promise you we're doing everything we can. It might be better if you forget about it for a little while. Okay, sweetheart?"

Bryony tried, but you would be amazed how many books have brothers in them. She decided it was time to make a big sacrifice.

"Mum, Dad," she announced, "I've decided I don't mind."

"Don't mind what, darling?" asked her father, removing spaghetti sauce from his tie. "Do you have to wave your spoon about so much?"

"I don't mind about having a brother," said Bryony. "I've thought about it a lot and I've decided that it's okay not to have one."

"Well, we're very happy as we are, aren't we?" said Mr. Beales, glancing at his wife. "Mummy and I think we're lucky to have *you*, Bryony. If it's going to be just the three of us, then that's fine, isn't it?"

"Oh, no, that's not what I meant!" cried the little girl.

"But you just said…"

"No! I meant I didn't mind after all if it's a sister," said Bryony. "I didn't want one at first because I thought she'd always be trying to borrow my things and she might be prettier than me, but Rosa's sister is quite sweet, and not at all pretty. So I think it would be okay. If it's hard to get brothers, I think you should get us a sister instead."

"We'll bear it in mind," said Mrs. Beales, not knowing whether to laugh or cry. "It's a bit like a lucky dip, actually, Bry. You get what you get. We'll see."

But still nothing happened. Bryony started school and was busy with her new friends. Then Rosa had *another* sister, which brought the whole subject up again.

"It doesn't seem fair," said Bryony. "How come some people have lots of babies and others don't?"

"That's a very good question, " said her mother, "but we'll have to wait until you're a bit older before we talk about that some more. Everyone's different, that's all. You are different from Rosa, and I am different from Rosa's mummy."

A year later, on a fine spring day, Bryony went out into the country with her mother and father for a picnic. They all sat down on top of a hill and spread out

the cloth with sandwiches, cakes, crisps and fruit.

"We wanted to have a special picnic," said Bryony's mum, "because we've got some really exciting news to tell you. Next month, just after your birthday, you're going to have..."

"A brother! A brother!" cried Bryony. "Or is it a sister? Oh, no it isn't either. You aren't fat at all, mummy. Oh, it's something else."

She looked so sad that her dad scooped her up for a big hug.

"It isn't a brother," he said. "It's *two* brothers! Mummy and I tried to have a baby for us all but we couldn't. These little boys—they're called Billy and Jo—need a new family. They're going to come and live with us. Billy is only two, but Jo is nearly as old as you are."

Bryony had often imagined this moment. She thought it would make her very happy. But this was different from what had happened to her friends. It was a bit worrying.

"Will they be *real* brothers?" she asked. "Will they stay all the time? Will they think I'm their sister?"

"They will certainly be real brothers," her dad reassured her, "and they will stay with us all the time. They already know they are going to have a new sister and they are very excited."

Bryony grinned.

"That's all right, then," she said. "Hurry up and eat, Dad, I've got a lot to get ready back at home."

Over the next month, Bryony helped her parents get the boys' room ready. She brought in some of her old toys for Billy and helped Dad to choose some new toys as well. She got a few presents herself, which was good too.

She couldn't wait for her brothers to arrive.

The next few weeks were awful for Bryony. Billy pulled her hair and sat on her doll's house. Jo threw her teddy in the pond and laughed at her because she couldn't swim yet. After only a few days, Bryony suggested strongly to her mother that the boys were sent back.

"No, Bry, they just need a bit of time to settle down," said her mum. "And Jo is only having a laugh. He's great, isn't he? I expect he'll help you with swimming if you ask him."

But Jo splashed Bryony and tried to drown her. At least, that's what *Bryony* said. He tried to scare her with plastic spiders, too, and was cross when it didn't work. Bryony began to wonder why she had *ever* thought that brothers were a good idea.

Very gradually, Bryony grew fond of Billy. Even more gradually, she and Jo became friends. Bryony decided that brothers were okay after all. She had only wanted *one* brother, but two were just about bearable.

"No more brothers, though!" she told her mum.

Her mother laughed and said, "It's a deal, Bry!"

It was just over a year later, at Christmas, that Bryony's parents broke the news that another baby was expected.

"We're as surprised as you are," said her mum, "and yes, Bry, this time I will get fat."

A few weeks later, at supper, Mrs. Beales, looking flushed and excited, had more news to tell.

"I'm going to get *very* fat!" she said. "It isn't one baby. It's three! There are going to be *six* children in this house!"

Bryony and Jo exchanged a glance. For the first time, Bryony felt that they were thinking exactly the same thing.

Later, at the end of the garden, Jo said, "We'll just have to stick together, that's all. You and me, sister."

"Let's hope they're girls," said Bryony. "Two brothers are enough for me—easily."

"One brother is enough for me," said Jo with feeling. "On the other hand, one sister is enough, too."

This time, it didn't seem a very long wait. Mum had to stay in bed for the last few weeks before the babies were born, so when she was whisked off to the hospital at last, it didn't seem odd not to have her at the table.

"Our last meal in peace," said Jo, gloomily.

"Our last evening without wailing and whining," said Bryony.

Their Dad came to find them a couple of hours later.

"They're here!" he said, grinning all over his face. "You can come and see them this afternoon. We're going to call them Robert, David and James. What do you say to that, Bryony B?"

"There's only one thing I can say," groaned Bryony. "Oh, brother!"

Mr. Mumbles' Magic Feast

Mr. Mumbles was a magician—a very good magician. He didn't do tricks. He did real magic that made his neighbours gasp and feel dizzy. That, to be fair, wasn't completely because they were so astonished by the brilliance of Mr. Mumbles' magic. You see, Mr. Mumbles had a most unfortunate sense of humour. He thought it was hilarious to up-end his friends in a huge vat of banana jelly or hang them by their braces on the weather vane of the village church. It was great to

be in the audience of one of Mr. Mumbles' Magic Shows, but awful if you happened to be someone plucked out to take part in one of the magician's spectacles.

Frankly, it's always a problem when a person with magic powers thinks he or she is funny. Ordinary practical jokes played by ordinary people are bad enough, but when someone with a sense of silliness can use magic to make the daftest idea come true, then everyone has to look out. Practical *magical* jokes can go too far.

Mr. Mumbles went too far much too often. In the time that he had lived in Spellville, there had been more different inhabitants of the houses on either side than most hotels see in a year. It's not much fun to live in a house and not know if a tide of purple custard is about to roll over the fence. Or to wake to find that every single item in your home has been turned upside down in the night.

One poor family moved house so quickly that their eldest son was *still* a parrot when they left—and probably still is to this day.

Of course, some brave souls have tried to tackle Mr. Mumbles on the subject. He's not a malicious man. He only means to have fun. It's just that Mr. Mumbles' idea of fun included turning dogs into hippopotamuses.

The first person to try to get Mr. Mumbles to see the error of his ways was old Lady Lollipop. She was a rich and powerful person in the town, who was appalled when she found that her long-serving (and long-suffering!) maid had been turned into a penguin. (Well, she always wore black and white and she waddled, so Mr. Mumbles didn't think it would make much of a difference. Penguins, however, are appallingly bad at carrying trays of early-morning tea!)

Lady Lollipop marched straight down to see Mr. Mumbles, all too conscious that she had had to put on her own hat (penguins are not too nifty at that either) and wasn't very good at such technical operations.

Mr. Mumbles was sitting in his garden, perfecting a spell to turn wedding cakes into armadillos. It was unfortunate, perhaps, that Lady Lollipop's hat looked quite so much like a wedding cake or that she had a life-long allergy to armadillos. The lady came out in blue spots and ran home screaming, the armadillo clinging to her head every step of the way. The only good thing to come out of all this was that the penguin and the armadillo became great friends and were often to be seen trotting down the road, hand in hand, on a summer's afternoon.

Mr. Blenkins at the bank was the next person to try to bring Mr. Mumbles to heel. He nearly had a heart attack when the magician came in one day and suggested (only half as a joke) that it would be an easy matter to change all the banknotes in the place into birthday cards.

"What for?" gasped Mr. Blenkins, trying to come to terms with the enormity of the catastrophe Mr. Mumbles was suggesting—and failing completely. He felt ill just about where his breakfast was sitting minding its own business.

"Oh, just for fun, you know!" laughed Mr. Mumbles. "I could turn them all back again in an instant—probably!"

Mr. Blenkins found himself as near to begging as a bank manager is ever likely to get. He offered Mr. Mumbles special terms on his account in return for a total lack of magic inside the bank. Mr. Mumbles, delighted at the effect he was having, accepted the deal.

It's a pity that Mr. Blenkins didn't consider the small print of the agreement as closely as he always advised his clients to do. Mr. Mumbles kept to his word. He didn't do a thing *inside* the bank. But when Mr. Blenkins arrived at work the next morning, he was apalled to see that the words "Spellville Central Bank", three feet high above the bank's massive doors, had mysteriously become "Smellville Central Bank".

Mr. Blenkins took the precaution of visiting Mr. Mumbles at the magician's home. He didn't want to tempt the spellmaker by showing him the inside of the bank again.

"Look here," said Mr. Blenkins, "this can't go on, you know. Some of the townsfolk are frightened to go out of their houses in case you turn them into ostriches or put raccoons on their heads.

"I have never, in my whole magical career, turned someone into an ostrich or put a raccoon on her head," said Mr. Mumbles loftily and, in fact, truthfully.

"I'm talking about the principle of the thing," replied Mr. Blenkins through clenched teeth. "Poor Lady Lollipop has retired to the coast to get over her ordeal. She thought it would be more comfortable for her pen... for her maid as well. That means she is no longer using the bank, Mr. Mumbles. It's not good for business at all."

Mr. Mumbles simply laughed.

"I promise you, Mr. Blenkins," he said, "that I will never ever turn you into a penguin or put an armadillo on your head. How's that? I'm a man of my word, you know."

Mr. Blenkins knew exactly what this meant and was not deceived.

"I would simply like to suggest that you confine your magic to entertainment," he said. The whole town loves your shows. It's just when they make people uncomfortable that you lose fans. What if you just used your considerable talents for amusing us all?"

"Well, all the things I do amuse *me*," replied Mr. Mumbles, "and I'm sorry that so few of my neighbours are able to take a joke. However, I can see that you think there is bad feeling in the town, and I don't want that. I'll give it some thought."

Mr. Mumbles put on his thinking cap, which was old and home to several spiders and a small bird, and did some serious … well, thinking. He didn't want everyone to dislike him, even if he did consider they were making a big fuss about nothing. What could he do to put things right? Suddenly, Mr. Mumbles had a Big Idea. The bird flew up in alarm and even the spiders scuttled into his ears for shelter. When Mr. Mumbles had a Big Idea, the thinking hat got very hot.

A week later, every person in Spellville found a purple envelope in his or her mail. Inside was a gilt-edged card on which an exciting invitation was printed.

The date was two weeks away. For the next thirteen days, Mr. Mumbles' Feast was the *only* subject on everyone's lips in Spellville. And the big question that old ladies were asking their maids, young ladies were asking their boyfriends, and little boys were asking their dogs was:

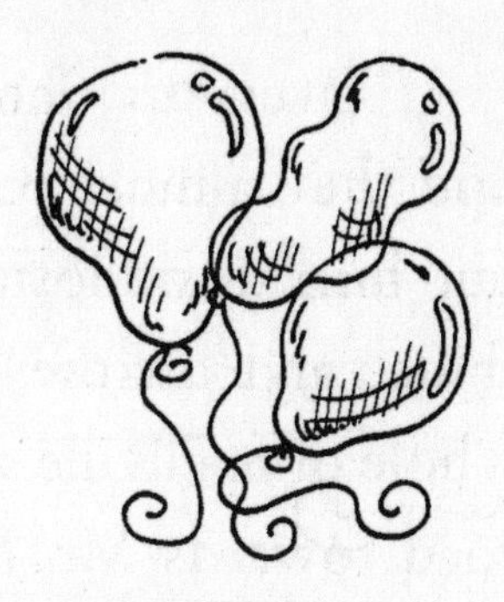

"Are you going?" Because, let's face it, anything to do with Mr. Mumbles is a risky business at the best of times.

"What if he's planning to tie us to balloons and let us float away?" asked one stout matron who would have needed a balloon the size of a house to get her off the ground. Her friends were kind enough not to point this out.

"What if the food is magic and makes us all start talking Chinese?" asked a little girl. Her mother crisply pointed out that as long as *everyone* was talking Chinese, it wouldn't matter in the least.

"Is it safe to take the baby?" an anxious woman asked her husband.

"Is it safe to take *me*?" he replied. "That's what I wonder."

Everyone had doubts. Everyone *said* they almost certainly would not go, but human curiosity is a very powerful thing, and on the day of the Feast, the whole of Spellville was trooping down the road towards Mr. Mumbles' house in its very best clothes.

Meanwhile, Mr. Mumbles was relaxing by his swimming pool, aware that several hundred people were about to descend on him, but not in any kind of pre-party tizz.

"That," he said to himself, "is the beauty of magic. It doesn't take any time at all. In fact, almost before you've thought of a spell, it has happened."

As the sound of excited chatter and clomping feet grew nearer and nearer to Mr. Mumbles' gate, the magician stood up at last and waved his hands vaguely in the direction of the house. *Poof piff paff!*

At once a hundred balloons bobbed into the sky, attached to trees, fences and arches. Flags waved gaily from open windows, while on the grass, long trestle tables, groaning with goodies, appeared in a flash. There were silken cushions under the trees, benches and easy chairs for the older folk to sit on, a bouncy castle for the children and penguins everywhere.

Yes, penguins. Mr. Mumbles couldn't help trying to have a joke.

The people of Spellville, crowding through the gate, oohed and aahed at the pretty sight that met their eyes. Some of the children, fed up with having to wear their best and most uncomfortable clothes, dived straight for the buns and disappeared under the tables. The older people, collapsing gratefully into chairs, were only too happy to accept tea and lemonade—even from penguins. Mr. Mumbles smiled. Since hearing about the difficulties of Lady Lollipop, he had put quite a bit of thought into the best way to train penguins to hold trays properly and not drop iced fancies into the laps of the landed gentry.

Half an hour passed. An hour passed. Everyone was having a lovely time. Mr. Mumbles passed among his guests, shaking hands and being as polite as he knew how. Very, very gradually, the visitors relaxed. Nothing horrible had happened yet. Maybe they had been wrong about Mr. Mumbles after all. He wasn't such a bad chap. And Lady Lollipop very often did make a fuss about nothing. These penguins were fun! Every home should have one!

By three o'clock, some of the older guests were dozing in the shade. The youngsters were playing a huge game of chase on the vast lawns. The penguins

were making sure that everything was kept clean and tidy and that full plates of cakes, sandwiches and sausage rolls kept coming to replace the empty ones. A polar bear was carrying around a large tray with ice creams and iced lollies. A small band struck up, with an orang-utan on violin, a sheep on drums and a most elegant parrot singing suitable summer songs.

Yes, everything was lovely. The Feast was a tremendous success. Even Mr. Blenkins the bank manager began to feel at ease.

But Mr. Mumbles was, frankly, bored. And I can't tell you how dangerous a bored magician can be. You simply never, ever want to be anywhere near a magician who has time on his hands and—as in the case of Mr. Mumbles—an unreliable sense of humour.

It was the penguins who gave Mr. Mumbles the idea. Very, very slowly, the visitors began to reach for their cardigans and cuddle into their coats as the temperature very, very slowly dropped. There didn't seem to be any reason for it. The sun was shining as brightly as ever and there was no breeze.

Mr. Mumbles rubbed his hands with glee (and to keep them warm) as one by one the visitors stood up and started walking around to keep warm. Much to everyone's astonishment, the swimming pool and the lake began to ice over. Before they could gather their wits, the guests were astonished to see six penguins and the polar bear giving a virtuoso skating display on the swimming pool.

Mr. Mumbles was charm itself.

"I can't imagine what is happening to the weather," he said, handing around blankets to those whose noses looked bluest or who were shivering so much they could not applaud the skating.

Only Mr. Blenkins had the presence of mind to think coldly (it was, in fact, impossible to think in any other way!) about the situation. The more he thought about it, the more certain he was that Mr. Mumbles was responsible for the big freeze. He hurried off to find his host.

Mr. Mumbles was just wondering whether to make it snow when Mr. Blenkins found him. The bank manager was a clever man but a logical one. The whole business of magic made him anxious and apprehensive. But as he saw Mr. Mumbles standing there, he suddenly realized that this was not a problem about magic. This was a problem about a bored and lonely man. If Mr. Mumbles had not been a magician, he would have been the kind of person to put plastic poached eggs on your plate and plastic spiders in your cereal. Because he had magical powers, his jokes were more extreme, that was all.

So as Mr. Blenkins shivered his way towards Mr. Mumbles, he didn't prepare an angry speech or fall on his knees and beg for better weather. Instead, he laughed … as heartily as he could manage with his teeth chattering.

"Ho ho ho! Ha ha ha! Well done, Mumbles!" he chortled.

Mr. Mumbles turned towards him with a look of such amazed delight on his face that Mr. Blenkins knew he had been right about the man.

"Do you like it?" he asked, like a little boy showing off his new train. "It's funny, isn't it? I got the idea from the penguins, you see."

"It's brilliant!" said Mr. Blenkins warmly (as far as his voice was concerned) and very coldly (as far as the rest of him was concerned), "and I'll tell you what would be even better." He whispered into Mr. Mumbles' ear.

So that is how, on the same afternoon, Spellville experienced sunny summer weather, Arctic conditions, and a tropical heatwave that caused a jungle to grow up around the magician's house. When they realized that nothing terrible was going to happen, the guests loved it. Before long, grannies were casting off their cardigans and going swimming in their vests and bloomers.

Mr. Blenkins was a sensible man. Most of the town was a client of his one way or another. Before the week was out, he had explained to everyone how to deal with Mr. Mumbles. All of a sudden, the folk of Spellville could see the advantages of having a magician in their midst instead of the disadvantages. And Mr. Mumbles was delighted to find that he was the most popular person in the place.

Only Lady Lollipop, hearing of events by phone from her seaside stay, had her doubts. But then she also still had an untrained penguin, so perhaps that is understandable!

Don't Jump, Jiggles!

An ostrich egg is enormous. Luckily, mother ostriches, who have to lay them, are pretty big, too. When Olga the ostrich laid her very first egg she was justly proud. It was large. It was smooth. It looked exactly as an egg should do. Olga called round all her friends and relatives to show them how clever she'd been to lay it.

"When you've laid as many eggs as I have," sighed her mother, "you won't be so chipper. They're a tie, eggs. You can't go out in the evening and leave them by themselves in case they get cold. They need watching all the time. And, of course, when they hatch it's even worse. Then your life's not your own. Still, it *is* a nice egg. I'm looking forward to being a granny at last."

Many of Olga's friends were equally unimpressed.

"Doesn't it *do* anything?" asked Simon, giving the egg an experimental kick. Olga stared at him coldly.

"You didn't do anything when you were in an egg, Simon," she said. "To be frank you don't do very much now. And please don't kick my egg."

Olga was looking forward to motherhood, on the whole. Life on the wide savannah was all very well, but there wasn't a lot to do. You could kick dust. You could run about a bit and worry a wildebeest. You could sit down

on the ground and pretend to be asleep (and keep one eye open for lions). But that was it, really. Olga thought it would be fun to teach a young ostrich all he or she needed to know. And when her youngster was old enough not to need her any more, she could lay another egg and start again.

Time seemed to pass very slowly on the savannah. Olga had begun to worry that all was not well with her egg, when one day she heard a little tapping sound and a crack appeared in the egg.

Olga watched eagerly as first a little orange beak and then a damp little head poked out of the egg, took a look around, and promptly popped back inside again.

Olga was a little startled. This wasn't supposed to happen, surely? She waited for a minute or two, but there was no more activity from the egg. Olga decided that it was time to intervene.

"Hello in there!" she called, looking down into the open egg.

"Go away!" said a little voice.

"But darling, it's your mummy here!" cooed Olga in her best maternal tones. "I'm so looking forward to getting to know you."

"No!" called the voice, and it sounded crosser than a dear little baby of any species had any right to be.

"You can't stay in there!" Olga tried to sound encouraging. "There is so much for you to do out here! It's lovely! Come and see!"

Even as she said these words, Olga felt a pang of conscience. As she gazed across the dusty plain, it was hard to summon up much enthusiasm for it. She understood completely when the little creature said from within the egg, "It isn't lovely. I had a look. It's dusty and boring. I'd rather stay here."

"You can't stay there," Olga said gently. "You need to eat, little one, and there is no more food for you in the egg. Come on. It will be okay. Really."

The baby ostrich was stubborn, but he wasn't stupid. He poked his head cautiously out of the egg again, looked around, shuddered, sighed, and slowly clambered out, shaking his skinny little legs.

Olga's heart filled with pride. Something about the little ostrich's jerky movements gave her an idea.

"I'm going to call you Jiggles," she said. "Is that okay?"

Jiggles jiggled.

"It's not bad," he said. "Where is everyone? It's not just you and me, is it?"

"No, we've got lots of friends and relatives," said Olga, "and, of course, your dad would love to be here but he bumped his beak trying to chase a Land Rover and has been taken to the animal hospital until he gets better. He'll be back before long, I expect. He's a bit accident prone. He once broke his leg kicking a warthog (they're a lot more solid than giraffes) and he lost a lot of feathers that time he tangled with a porcupine. But you'll like him when he comes back."

"What is there to eat, then?" asked Jiggles, looking with disfavour at the dusty ground and the few sparse trees on the horizon.

"Seeds," replied his mother, "leaves, fruit if you can find it, shoots if they come up, flowers if it rains, and insects if you can catch them."

"It's not what you would call a gourmet selection, is it?" commented Jiggles, scratching in the dust as a little ant ran by. "But, hmmm, ants aren't bad."

Over the next few days, Olga showed her youngster off to everyone she met, and even they were impressed by Jiggles' bright little eyes, sharp little tongue and fast little legs. He could run like the wind, soon leaving poor old Olga gasping as she trotted after him.

It was late one evening, as the sun set, red and round, over the savannah, that Jiggles asked the question that Olga was to come to dread over the months that followed that evening.

"When do I learn to fly" asked the young ostrich. "I reckon I'm ready, but I don't know what to do."

"That's because you can't. Fly, I mean," said Olga.

"Can't? Why not?"

"Ostriches don't. Other birds fly, Jiggles. But ostriches simply don't. Maybe we did once, but not for thousands and thousands of years, I think. None of us flies. Honestly. You ask anyone."

Jiggles had a look of deep disbelief on his face. Over the next few weeks, he did ask anyone. In fact, he asked everyone, including an astonished leopard who was so stunned to be being asked a question by someone who looked like breakfast that he didn't even try to catch Jiggles.

Jiggles soon found that everyone was in agreement.

"Vultures fly," yawned a lion cub, "and parrots and flamingoes. But ostriches don't. I'm very glad, myself."

"Why?" asked a startled Jiggles.

"Because of accidents," said the lion cub. "Think how dangerous it would be if something as big as an ostrich suddenly fell on you out of the sky. You wouldn't stand a chance."

"It wouldn't be all that great for the ostrich, either," said Jiggles coldly. "It doesn't seem to me that it's a good enough reason not even to try."

So Jiggles tried. He reasoned that ostriches must have wings for some reason. He ran along the ground, flapping as hard as he could, and frightened a number of gazelles into moving home, but he didn't leave the ground.

Next, Jiggles tried jumping off anthills. The ants didn't like it, but Jiggles didn't care. Over and over again, his large feet clambered up the anthill. Over and over again, his even larger body fell with a thud on the ground the other side.

In the end, an elderly elephant, who had an even larger body, came to have a word with young Jiggles, who was now almost as big as his mother and whose feathers were gradually becoming shiny black and white.

"Jiggles," he said, "give it a rest, can't you? You're making the ground shake so much I can't tell when my ghastly sister is about to arrive. I like to have enough to time to disappear under the mud in the waterhole. Three times last week she crept up and caught me because you were making so much noise jumping off that anthill. What are you trying to achieve, lad?"

Jiggles explained. The elephant looked pained.

"Give it up, Jiggles," he said, "and give it up now. You are an ostrich and you will never leave the ground for as long as you live. Your father will be home soon. Ask him about it. He's tried most silly things in his time, but even he never tried to fly, I think."

Jiggles tried to look respectful. The elephant was *very* big. But the ostrich just couldn't believe he was being as silly as all that. He always came back to the same question. Why did he have wings if he wasn't meant to fly?

It was a week or so later that a film crew arrived on the savannah. Several of the animals were given starring roles in the movie that was being made. A senior lion even had a speaking (well, roaring) part. Much to his disgust, Jiggles was not needed. Apparently there were to be no ostriches at all in the film. Indeed, an annoying man with a handkerchief wrapped around his head kept coming along and telling the ostriches not to drop feathers all over the place, as it spoilt the look of things.

Jiggles was strongly tempted to kick the annoying man, but his mother dragged him away, saying, "It's that sort of behaviour that always gets your father into trouble. I expect better of you, young Jiggles!"

After that, the frustrated ostrich tried to ignore the film people, but it wasn't easy, especially when they erected a huge tower right in the middle of the plain. At the top of it, an intrepid cameraman was filming the backs of a herd of gazelles passing underneath.

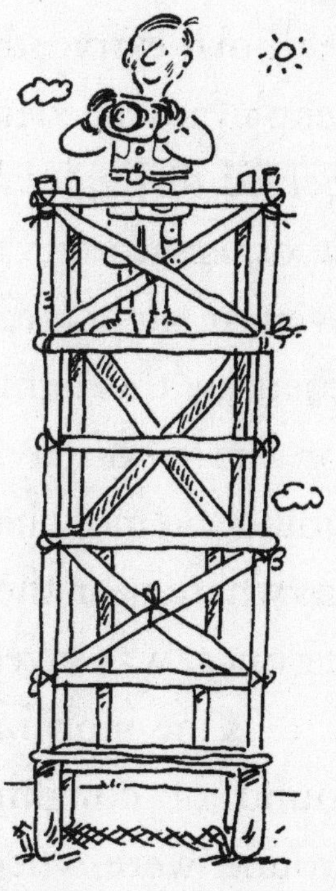

Gazelles are not the most intelligent creatures, and the shot had to be done time and time again. Meanwhile, Jiggles had suddenly seen the possibilities of the tower. If a fit and courageous bird (*with* wings) were to jump from the top, surely he would be high enough to start to fly? Jiggles made his plans.

An extraordinarily large number of people are needed to make a movie. It seemed to Jiggles as if there was someone or other around the tower all the time. Even at night, technicians were at work resetting the lights and checking scripts for the next day. It seemed that there would be no chance for Jiggles to get anywhere near the tower. But the ostrich, for once, was saved by the weather.

One morning, Jiggles awoke to the sound of coughing. Animals for miles around were wheezing and snorting as a duststorm swept over the plain. The movie crew were all hiding in their tents and trailers. Jiggles screwed up his eyes against the swirling dust and set off for the tower. His time had come.

It is very hard to climb ladders in a duststorm. It is almost impossible if you are an ostrich. The rungs are not made for big ostrich feet. The handrails are not designed for big ostrich wings. Above all, nothing human is meant to accommodate an ostrich's enormously long neck. Poor Jiggles really struggled as he made his perilous ascent.

Then, just as he neared the platform at the top, the duststorm suddenly settled as soon as it had begun. Jiggles looked out over the clear, sunlit savannah. It was perfect flying weather.

Of course, several animals and even more humans were looking out over the savannah as well. One of them happened to look up. There soon was not a living creature within twenty miles who did not know that a large ostrich was standing at the top of the scaffolding tower, preparing to jump.

Anxious relatives gathered around.

"Don't jump, Jiggles!" they cried.

Anxious moviemakers huddled in groups, trying to think of a sensible way to move a fully grown ostrich (for Jiggles

was almost grown-up now) from eighty feet up in the air.

Jiggles flapped his wings. He took a step nearer the edge. He decided to count to five.

One…

Two…

Three…

Four…

"*Don't do it, son!*" yelled a powerful voice that Jiggles had never heard before. It was his father!

Jiggles hesitated, and as he did so, his dad opened his wings wide and *charged* at the crowd at the foot of the tower. He made a terrifying sight. Animals, humans and quite a lot of dust scattered as he approached. He didn't, however, quite manage to stop before he reached the tower.

Boing!!!

As his father's newly mended beak came into sharp contact with the steel poles that formed the tower, Jiggles jiggled dangerously. Swaying over the ground far, far below, jumping suddenly didn't seem such a wonderful idea. Jiggles clung with all his might to the platform, until it stopped rocking. Then, while his father kept back the crowds below, he climbed slowly down the ladder.

Jiggles and his father had a lot of catching up to do, but first the older ostrich had a few words to say on the subject of wings and their uses.

"Run at anyone or anything with your wings out wide," said Jiggles' dad, "and they'll back down. It's brilliant. Better than flying any day. It's what wings are for, lad."

Jiggles was impressed.

"Anyone or anything?" he queried.

His dad had the grace to look a little embarrassed.

"Except Land Rovers," confessed the ostrich. "And I'd give warthogs and porcupines a wide berth, too, but that's just a personal thing. I'm glad to know you, son!"

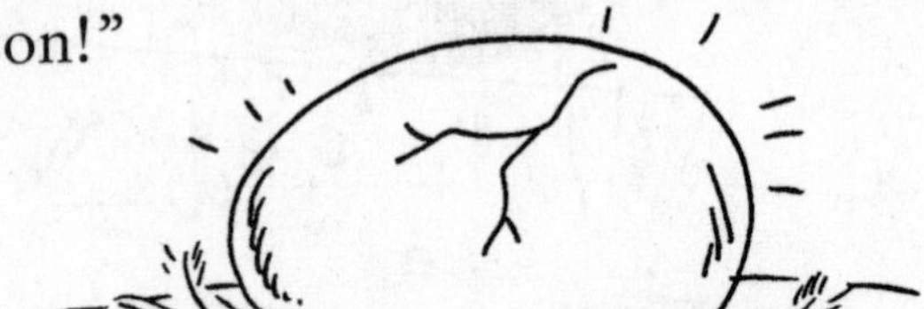

Mrs. Norton's Knitting

Some people collect stamps, or spot trains, or build model aircraft. There are those who paint horrible pictures and give them to all their friends. Most of us have a hobby of some kind, but Mrs. Norton's knitting was in a different class.

Mrs. Norton knitted from the moment she woke up in the morning to the moment her head touched the pillow at night. There were even rumours that she knitted in her sleep, but that was never proved. Ever since Mr. Norton had passed away ten years earlier, Mrs. Norton had lived alone with several thousand balls of wool and an array of knitting needles that looked like some kind of medieval torture machine when displayed together.

Now Mrs. Norton was a very enthusiastic knitter. She was a very quick knitter. But she wasn't a very *good* knitter. Her blankets usually had holes in them, and few people were persuaded by Mrs. Norton's protestations that they were part of a lacy pattern. Mrs. Norton's jumpers were no better. There was always one sleeve longer than the other, and neck holes were either so small that no one could pull them on or so loose that

wearers had been known to fall out of their sweaters as they walked along.

Mrs. Norton wasn't very good at choosing colours either. Her favourite combination was a deep cerise pink with lime green. She was quite fond of lilac and egg-yolk yellow, too. Best of all, Mrs. Norton liked to knit stripes. They were easy (although they still seemed to go wonky somehow) and they meant she could use all the different shades of wool she liked. Since Mrs. Norton even knitted in the dark if there was a power cut, she sometimes used shades she didn't like as well. But she could never, ever be accused of being tasteful.

Now, Mrs. Norton wasn't a great knitter but she was generous. She gave jumpers to all her friends. It was terribly easy to spot a Norton Knit from a hundred yards away. The stripes in horrible colours were a clue. The uneven arms and the neck problem only confirmed it. Mrs. Norton's neighbours didn't want to offend her. They tried to wear one of her jumpers once a year or so and make sure that she saw them. They tried to make sure that their other friends *didn't* see them!

A person only needs so many ugly striped sweaters. When she had knitted six sweaters each for everyone she knew, Mrs. Norton turned her needles to other

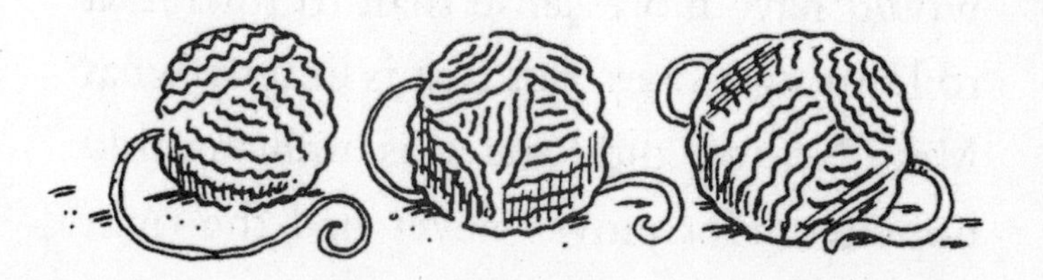

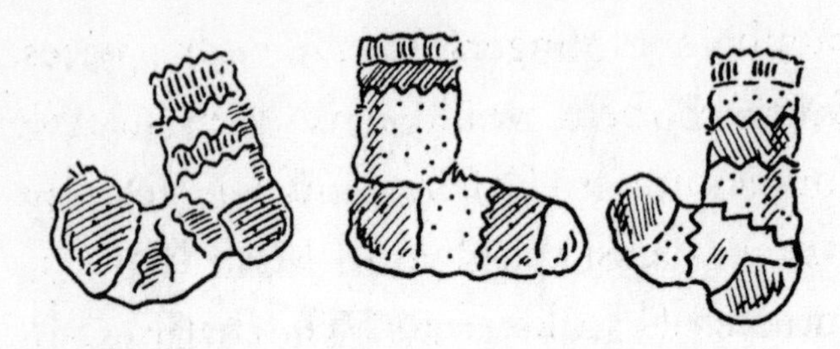

projects. She tried socks first, but it is terribly difficult to knit socks. They have heels that are tricky and toes that are testing. Mrs. Norton failed at every turn. She tried to pass off her efforts as leg-warmers for sheep, but the local farmers politely turned down her kind offers of free supplies. In the end, Mrs. Norton put away the socks in a deep cupboard and tried something else.

You might think that someone who has tried and failed to knit a decent sock would have more sense than to turn next to knitting gloves, but that is exactly what Mrs. Norton did. She was unbelievably hopeless. Her gloves never had the right numbers of fingers in the right places. Some of them would have been suitable for octopuses. Others would have made better socks than poor Mrs. Norton's intentional socks, if you see what I mean.

Mrs. Norton liked a challenge, but she had to confess that gloves had her beaten. Surely, she thought, there must be something simpler in her favourite book: *One Thousand Fascinating Projects for Knitters with Nerve*.

There was. Over the next few weeks, Mrs. Norton's nearest and dearest each received two dozen egg-cosies, fifteen bobble-hats, a charming cover for their toilet paper in the shape of a giraffe in a

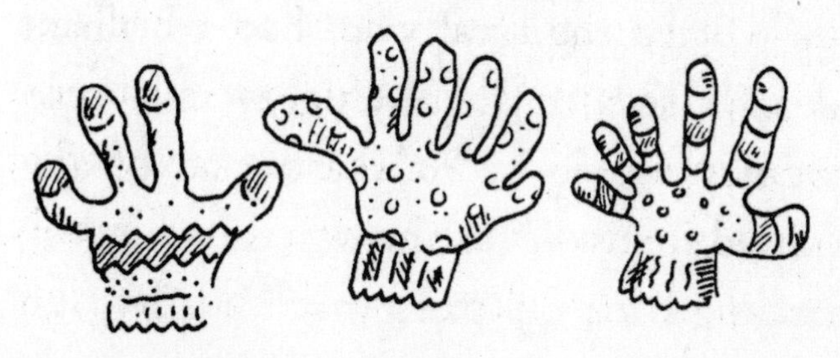

waistcoat, and some knitted underpants. If you think about it, few things are less appealing than knitted underpants, and several of Mrs. Norton's neighbours took this as a sign that it was time they tried to wean her from knitting and find her another hobby.

It was an effort that was doomed before it began. Mrs. Norton never put down her knitting for long enough to *listen* to another idea, let alone to try it out. She would stare vaguely at her companion and say, "Sorry, what was that? I came to a complicated bit just then and couldn't concentrate on what you were saying."

Then the local vicar had a brilliant idea. It seemed that refugees in a cold country would be only too glad of any knitted items—even, he dared to suggest, handing back the pairs that Mrs. Norton had thoughtfully decorated with a cross—knitted underpants.

Mrs. Norton was very happy to hear that there was another outlet for her talents. She felt sorry for the freezing refugees and tried to knit faster than ever. Unfortunately, faster knitting meant more mistakes. Knitted underpants really shouldn't have more than two legs. Knitted hats should not be as big as buckets. Mrs. Norton felt sure they would prove useful for *something*, but she wasn't sure what.

The vicar had a large barn next to his vicarage where village fêtes were held if it was wet. Despite torrential rain the following summer, the vicar seemed strangely reluctant to open his barn and usher the merrymakers inside. Of course, he knew, as the others did not, that several bales of knitting, rejected even by the freezing refugees, were to be found inside. He simply could not bear to hurt Mrs. Norton's feelings by showing her how her handiwork had been received.

Now Mrs. Norton was such a demon knitter that she didn't put her needles down long enough to do any of the ordinary things of life. She didn't, for example, cook herself proper meals, but snacked on biscuits and crisps between rows. She didn't get as much sleep as she should either, as she always wanted to get just one more section finished before bed.

This meant that she was very often knitting into the early hours. Naturally, Mrs. Norton had no time for check-ups at the doctor's or healthy walks or changes of scene.

So perhaps it wasn't very surprising that Mrs. Norton became very ill. She had ignored the signs for years, and when she finally collapsed in a tangle of wool on her kitchen floor, she had to be rushed to hospital at once.

Luckily, a proper diet, rest and peace and quiet were all that Mrs. Norton needed. The doctor at the hospital was strict. No work of any kind. Gentle exercise. Good food. Lots of visits to friends and relatives. That was the recipe for Mrs. Norton.

Mrs. Norton felt like a car without wheels. It seemed so strange to have nothing at all to do with her hands. When she got home, she found that kind friends had removed every last scrap of wool and even her tiniest needles. She was so desperate, she even wondered if she could knit with wooden spoons and string, but she found that these had been taken away as well! Mrs. Norton sat in her house and felt very unhappy. In fact, she felt just the way she would have after her husband died if she had not had her knitting to keep her occupied.

As Mrs. Norton struggled with her feelings, the vicar was struggling with his barn door. As all Mrs. Norton's knitting equipment, plus the refugees' returned garments, plus several hundred knitted items that villagers had kindly given him (and each one bearing the unmistakable mark of Mrs. Norton's skills) were stored in his barn, he could hardly shut the door.

Now that she was no longer knitting, Mrs. Norton had time to do the normal things that most of us do. She read the paper and magazines. She watched television and listened to the radio. She found out, in other words, just exactly what was going on in the world outside—far from weird woollies and odd egg-cosies. She was amazed.

"Did you know," Mrs. Norton asked her neighbour over the fence one morning, "that navy blue is *the* colour for mascara this year?"

The neighbour was stunned.

"Mascara?" she queried. "Do you mean merino, or perhaps mohair?"

"What? Those are kinds of wool!" cried Mrs. Norton. "You couldn't wear those on your eyelashes! Are you feeling quite well, dear? You should take it a little easier, like me."

When the vicar came to call, Mrs. Norton was eager to see him.

"I want you to try this spaghetti recipe," she cried. "I haven't done much cooking in recent years, so it will need a bit of fine tuning, but it tastes good."

The visitor was presented with something that looked suspiciously like some of Mrs. Norton's knitting, especially when he tried to wrap it around his fork.

It did, however, as she said, taste pretty good, especially coming from a cook who had not picked up a pan for ages.

Over the next few weeks, Mrs. Norton devoured daytime television and magazines of all kinds. She had a go at everything from model railway building (not a huge success) to cake decorating (interesting if you like modern art or are a fan of the way that building sites look after a demolition team has been in).

When she wasn't up to her elbows in glue or frosting, Mrs. Norton made some alarming experiments with make-up, and revealed that her colour sense for this was very similar to the skill she showed in choosing shades for knitting.

Mrs. Norton's cooking also became more adventurous. She delighted her friends and relatives with exotic dishes from around the world. Very few were identifiable on the plate, and Mrs. Norton's vagueness didn't help.

"Well," she would say, looking hopefully at a green and orange mixture lying like a cow pat in the middle of her plate, "this might be orange and pistachio mousse. On the other hand, it could be pea and squash medley. I can't remember what I tried in the end."

Tasting often revealed that Mrs. Norton's changes of heart occurred somewhere in the *middle* of a recipe, so

that visitors found themselves eating, say, orange and pea surprise.

One day, when Mrs. Norton was rushing through the village on her way to buy equipment for corn-dolly making, she met her friend Mrs. Stevens. Mrs. Norton looked with distress at the jumper her friend was wearing.

"Is business bad?" she asked with great sympathy. "Are you shopping in the charity shops, now? And if I may say so, my dear, purple and green with red stripes are not particularly good colours for you, not with an olive skin tone."

Mrs. Stevens was astonished.

"But Marla, my dear," she cried, "you knitted me this ... er ... *beautiful* jumper yourself last winter. Don't you remember?"

Mrs. Norton firmly denied all knowledge of the offending article, but as she walked back to her cottage, she did begin to remember. And as she walked, her face became pinker and pinker. She recalled now that quite a lot of mis-shapen articles had left her needles. Strangely, with so many new interests, she felt no need to take up knitting again, but she did feel a little embarrassed about the amount of knitwear with which she had showered her poor friends. Mrs. Norton was thinking so hard about this that she walked right into the vicar, who had been on his way to see her.

"Well, this is lucky," said the vicar, as he picked himself up off the road. "How are you, my dear Mrs. Norton?"

"As a matter of fact," replied the lady, "I'm feeling rather bad about something, but I don't know what to do about it."

"Something you've done?" asked the vicar. "Or something you haven't done, my dear?"

"Oh, something I've done!" cried Mrs. Norton. "Lots and lots of things I've done! I just don't know what to do to put things right."

"An apology?" suggested the vicar gently. "It can work wonders. Maybe if you told me what is troubling you..."

Mrs. Norton told him.

The vicar hesitated. Should he risk it? Then he told her about his barn full of knitted goods.

"If you can help me to find a home for them," he said, "I think we can call the whole chapter closed, Mrs. Norton. It is so good to see you looking happier again."

Mrs. Norton didn't hesitate.

"Recycling!" she cried. "I've been reading a lot about it recently."

The vicar looked dubious. "But I'm not sure anyone would want to wear..."

"No, no!" cried his parishioner. "It's the fibres that can be used, not the garments themselves (not that you can call most of them *garments*, I'm afraid). They can be used to make felt or stuff cushions and all sorts of things. I'll find an address for you."

Mrs. Norton was right. Not only was a company happy to come and take the awful objects off the vicar's hands, they even paid him money.

"The village fête will be better than ever this year!" he smiled. "And it's all down to you, Mrs. Norton. What would we do without you?"

Mrs. Norton blushed. "Perhaps you would like one of my handmade lampshades for the tombola," she said.

The vicar groaned. The knitting problem was solved, but there were so *many* crafts left!

My Special Santa

When I was little—and that's a long time ago now—I loved Christmas. That was mostly because my dad loved it, too. He told me once that when I was born, he thought straight away about he'd be able to take me carol-singing and do all the really Christmassy things. Mum likes Christmas too, of course, but she isn't such a kid about it as Dad is. He'd dress up like a reindeer in a second if someone was daft enough to give him the costume.

We had a strict rule in our house. No Christmas until the first day of December. That was because Mum's birthday was on the last day of November, and she insisted that we celebrated that *before* we started making a fuss about the festive season.

Poor Mum. It was such torture for me and Dad, long after there were decorations in the shops, not to be able to put up tinsel or go shopping.

"Miss my birthday, and you'll be doing the cooking on Christmas Day," warned Mum in her deepest voice. Dad's great, but he couldn't cook a turkey to save his life. There wasn't any choice, really.

So Christmas started for me and Dad on December 1st, and it started with lists. We both made a list for Santa. Mine had things like a doll's house and a new bike. Dad's had things like a Harley-Davidson and four months holiday in the Caribbean. Personally, I thought he'd be better off putting down something like socks and aftershave, but it was his list.

"Trust me," he said. "You've got to aim high with these things. One year, Santa's going to find himself with a few thousand left over from his present fund and he might just pick my list off the pile and say, 'Hey! This guy *deserves* a yacht. No problem.'"

I've heard that some people put their lists in the fire so that they float up the chimney to Santa. We didn't have a fire in our flat, and the year we tried putting them in the oven, Mum got a bit

unseasonal. So we used to take them to the letterboxes you see in department stores—the ones where they have a Santa sitting in a grotto or somewhere and giving out little presents to kids.

Each year, Dad claimed to know the box we should use.

"I've got inside information," he'd say, touching his nose significantly, "that this box will be the last to be emptied on Christmas Eve this year. Think about it.

Last emptied means top of the pile or the sack. It'll be the first to be read. There'll be much more chance of us getting what we put down."

I didn't think this worked with his getting-a-yacht argument, but I didn't like to say so. I didn't want to say anything that would stop Dad's eyes shining.

The first weekend in December, armed with our lists, Dad and I would go shopping. We'd made more lists by then, not of things we wanted to *get* but of things we wanted to *give*. This time, I must say Dad was a lot more realistic. I noticed there was no mention of yachts or four-month holidays on his list of things to buy for Mum.

"She gets seasick," he said, when I mentioned this.

Of course, parts of our lists were *secret*, even from each other. I didn't tell Dad what I was going to get for him, and he didn't tell me what he was looking at for me. For that, we each went shopping with Mum, but it wasn't half so much fun. Mum strode along and moaned about the crowds the whole time. Dad and I really *enjoyed* the jostling and shoving. If you're not in a hurry, it doesn't matter, and we loved to look at the Christmas decorations and the pretty, lighted windows before we hurried home as it grew darker. And if the crowds were too bad, Dad carried me on his shoulders. Then *I* got seasick.

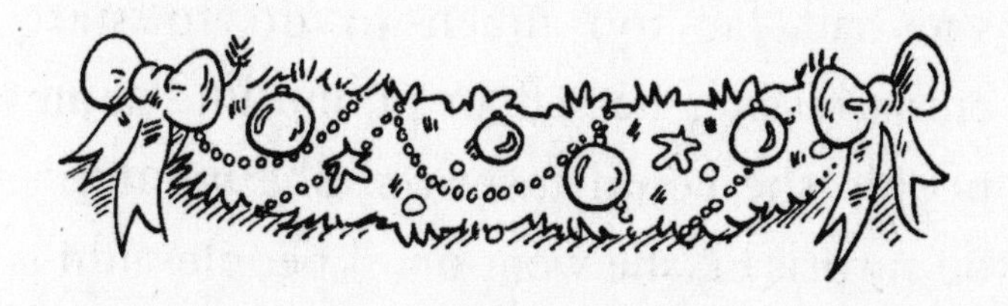

Sometime around the second week in December, we always went carol-singing with people from church. Mr. Kitchen played the trombone and nearly deafened us all. It was hard to tell if you were singing in tune with that many decibels slamming into your eardrums. As far as Dad was concerned, any tunefulness would have been a miracle. He sang at full volume in a way that was excruciatingly painful—or would have been if the trombone hadn't drowned out what he was doing. Now that I think back, maybe it wasn't coincidence that we were put in front of Mr. Kitchen year after year.

Mum didn't come carol-singing, although she's got a nice voice. She said she had far too much to do to start embarrassing herself in public like some people she could mention. She wouldn't be surprised, she went on, if people didn't pay us to *go away*. Dad said he didn't care why they paid us, as long as we could collect lots of money for the kids in hospital at Christmas. He said he couldn't imagine anything worse than being away from your family at such an important time of the year. Then he'd hug Mum and me and she'd tell him not to be soft.

The last few days before Christmas used to crawl by. When we'd bought all our presents, and wrapped them up, and hidden them, and then hidden them again in case someone had been peeping the first time, there always seemed to be a few days when nothing much happened at all. Mum was frazzled trying to do shopping and cooking and finishing work, so Dad and I kept out of the way. We tried to do things that kept us in a Christmassy mood, like skating or watching videos.

At last, ever so slowly, Christmas Eve came round. Mum would flop down at last and chat while Dad and I put up the Christmas tree. I know lots of people do it sooner, but Dad always insisted we had a real one, and he said it would start dropping its sharp little needles long before Christmas if we did it too soon. It was fun seeing the old, familiar decorations coming out of their tissue paper. The lights *never* worked, and it took ages for Dad to find out why, but that was part of the fun. We had a deal. I decorated the lower branches and Dad did

the top ones—except the angel on the very top. Dad held me up for that, and if some years she looked a bit wonky, it didn't really matter.

Then Mum would say, "Okay, young lady, time for bed."

I'd sit up in bed in the dark, trying to go to sleep, but nothing seemed to work. Each year, I worried and worried that Santa would realize I was awake and not come. But falling asleep is really hard if you keep thinking about it.

After I'd been in bed a couple of hours (although it seemed like days!), Dad would put his head around the door and say, "I think I can hear some sleigh-bells outside. Are you asleep?" And I'd say, "Yes, Dad!"

Mum had a firm rule that no presents could be opened before breakfast. When I was tiny, that was really hard. Then, one year, it suddenly occurred to me that if I *made* breakfast, I could start opening right away. Ten minutes later, my parents woke very suddenly in a shower of orange juice and milk, with crispy cereal in their ears.

"Ooops!" I said. It's funny how a rug that never gives you a moment's trouble normally can trip you up the minute you pick up a tray of food and drink. On that occasion, Mum was just about to get angry when Dad's giggles made her see the funny side. The fact that it was half past three in the morning may have had something to do with it. I was told to go back to bed while Mum and Dad cleared up. You wouldn't believe how long it took them to get the crispy cereal out of their ears.

We used to take turns opening our presents. Dad and I had lots of jokes. He'd pick up a very small parcel that was quite obviously handkerchiefs from Aunt Ellen, and I'd say, "What do you think it is, Dad?"

He'd shake the parcel to see if it rattled (it didn't), sniff it to see if it smelled (it didn't), poke it to see if it was squishy (it was). Then he'd look very solemn and say, "You know, Fiz, I think this might just be *it*. It's squishier than most yachts, of course, but you never know what they're doing these days with modern materials. You have a feel and see what you think."

I would prod the parcel until the paper started to tear.

"I don't think it's a yacht, Dad," I'd say, "but it's the right shape for a holiday in the Caribbean."

Then Mum would tell us that if we didn't get on with it, there wouldn't be any lunch, so Dad would tear off the paper pretending to be a savage dog.

"Oh," he'd say, "look, hankies! We were almost right, Fiz!"

After lunch, when we were almost too full to move, Dad always offered to do the washing up, and Mum always said it would take her three weeks to find things again if he did, so he should take me out into the garden to get some air for an hour or so.

It was hardly ever real Christmassy weather, with snow on the ground and frost in the trees, but we still used to peer closely at the paths as we crept along.

"Do you see any?" Dad would ask.

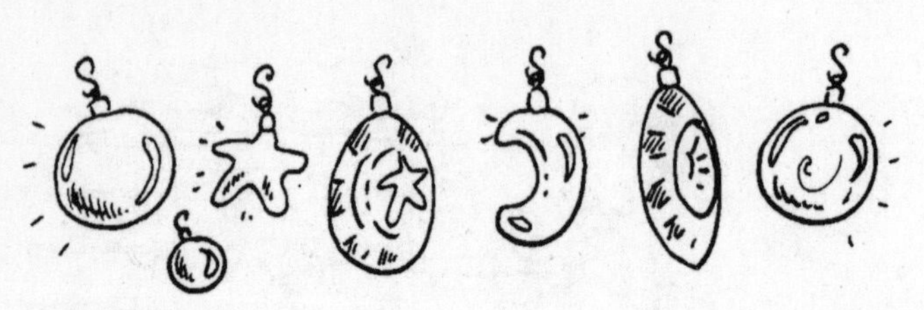

"I think I've got something here. Look!"

I'd bend down and examine the ground before shaking my head.

"No," I said, "it might be a cat or a dog, but it's not a reindeer print."

Then, later, Dad would say, "Look, partner! These are the genuine article. How long ago do you think this chap passed this way? Twelve hours? Ten?"

"Eleven and a half," I'd say.

When we'd tracked the reindeer as far as we could (we'd have got right to the North Pole if if hadn't been for the fact that those reindeer can *fly*), we'd feed the ducks on the pond and say "Merry Christmas" to them. I don't know if you've noticed how often ducks quack

"Merry Christmas" to each other. Only it sounds like "Quack, quack, *quack*, quack!" of course.

As the light began to fade, we hurried home for warm drinks and silly games, although Mum said she didn't know where we got the energy from when we'd been playing silly games all day. Then Dad would carry me up to bed and say, "Did you have a good Christmas, princess?"

And I'd say, "It was the best one ever, Dad!" And, you know, it always was.

But one Christmas wasn't like all the rest. Things started to go wrong back in the summer, when Dad's boss decided to retire. His son took over, but Dad said his heart wasn't really in it. By August, things were looking very bad. By the end of September, Dad was out of a job.

At first, Dad was hopeful that he'd soon find something else. But as the weeks passed and he was still going through the paper each morning with a red pen and a hopeful expression, he began to get a bit depressed.

"That's fifty-six applications," he told Mum, "and forty-nine letters saying

'Thanks, but no thanks.' Seven of them didn't even bother to reply."

"Just you wait, Dad, they'll be queuing up for a ride when you've got the yacht," I said, trying to cheer him up.

But Dad shook his head. "That doesn't seem so funny any more, Fiz. Let's not talk about it, okay?"

The autumn passed. Still there was no sign of a job for Dad. Mum increased her hours in the store and was very tired all the time. They started arguing about silly little things, like which brand of orange juice we should buy.

Then, just before Mum's birthday, Dad got a job.

"It's not much—only temporary," he told me, "but it's better than nothing. Only I'm going to be working long hours, Fiz, so I want you to be a good girl and look after your mum, okay?"

He was right about the long hours. He just never seemed to be at home any more. He didn't even make it home for Mum's birthday. She said she didn't mind and was just as happy to catch up on some sleep, but I could see she was upset, really.

Of course, after Mum's birthday, Dad and I usually only had one thing on our minds: Christmas! It was different this year. Dad wasn't at home the next weekend, so I asked Mum to help me write my lists. She didn't know how to do it properly at all.

"No, no!" I said, when I saw that she had written "bubble bath" and "tights" on her list. "You have to put something big, like a plane, or a racing car. That's what Dad always does."

"Sometimes I think your Dad doesn't live in the real world," said Mum.

There wasn't any carol-singing for us that year. When I mentioned that I would still like to go to Mum, she said she was sorry but she just didn't have time.

"And I should think everyone else will be relieved not to have your dad bellowing in their ears," she said.

Mum said we didn't have enough money to buy Christmas cards for all the people I wanted to send them to.

"You don't *need* to give one to the lady who sells newspapers, Fiz," she said. "Or Mrs. Budd next door. She's never

given us a card in all the years we've lived here. I bet some of these people on your list don't even know your name."

I didn't really think that mattered. Dad used to say that everyone likes a bit of Christmas cheer. It was hard not to notice that our own Christmas wasn't at all cheery this year.

As Mum wouldn't let me buy them, I decided to make my own cards. I ran out of red and green paint pretty quickly, and the silver markers from the year before had dried up, so some of my cards didn't look very Christmassy. Still, as Dad said, it's the thought that counts.

I hardly saw Dad at all these days. He always seemed to be at work, and

when he was back at home he was really tired. I wasn't even sure if we were going to have a proper Christmas. We hadn't done any of the usual things. One day, I felt so sad about it I burst into tears over breakfast. I don't know why, really.

Mum was so surprised, she put her elbow in her coffee, which made me laugh and her cross. When we'd cleared up, she asked me what the matter was—and I told her. It was difficult to put into words the fact that somehow all the jolliness had gone out of Christmas.

Mum sat me down on her lap and said she was sorry.

"Things are difficult right now," she said, "but I promise you we will have a proper Christmas, with a tree, and sleigh bells outside, and good things to eat. You and Dad can go and look for reindeer prints and we'll play silly games just as we always do. I'll have a word with Dad. I'm sure he has some special prizes in store for you. And even if he doesn't get his yacht this year, well, that won't be any different from any other year, will it? I mean, let's face it, what is he going to do with a yacht? We live two hundred miles from the sea. I'm sure he's never sailed anything larger than a toy boat in his life. And on top of everything, he gets seasick."

"He said that was *you*!" I laughed.

"Typical!" grinned Mum. "Now, let's make a plan for the rest of the days

before Christmas. I'm sure there are lots of jolly things we can do. Shall I do the writing, or will you?"

We had a great time making our plans. Mum said we couldn't go to the Christmas Ice Show or do any more shopping, but we wrote down times when I could help her make star-shaped biscuits and when she would help me to wrap up my presents. I felt a lot better after that.

As slowly as ever, the time passed. I worried that there wouldn't be many presents that year, but Mum gave me a quick peep under her bed, where quite a lot of interesting parcels were hidden. Then, at last, it was Christmas Eve.

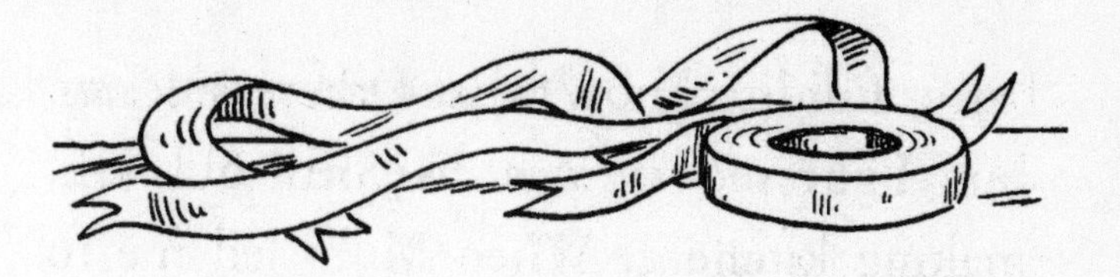

"Dad can't get away from work to help you decorate the tree today," Mum told me, "but I'll help you and then we can go and pick Dad up from work together. It'll be a surprise for him—and we'll all be together over Christmas, with no horrible old work or worries. Just us having a good time."

I nodded. It wasn't quite so much fun doing the tree with Mum, but I was just glad we'd got one at all. Dad had brought it home the evening before, when I was in bed. Mum wasn't tall enough to hold me up to put the angel on, but she said Dad would do it for me just this once.

"Now, hurry up," she said. "We've got to go and find your father. He finishes at six today."

I didn't know what Dad was doing, but I guessed it was like his old job, making kitchens. When Mum led me to the biggest, poshest store in town, I wondered what we were doing.

"It's just a little treat before we go home with Dad," she said. "There's someone here who would like to see you."

She led me to the special grotto that had been made for Santa to sit in, and for once there weren't any queues or people shoving. I hoped Dad had remembered to post our lists today, as he promised.

It's hard not to feel Christmassy when you're sitting on Santa's knee and talking about important things like presents. And this was a really nice Santa. He had twinkly brown eyes, like Dad, and when he said, "Ho, ho, ho! Merry Christmas!" it reminded me a lot of what was wrong with Dad's singing. Suddenly,

I grabbed Santa's beard and pulled! Someone very familiar grinned back.

Somehow, that Christmas was better than ever. Mum gave Dad a tiny plastic yacht and Dad gave Mum a diamond ring out of a cracker. Then, just after Boxing Day, Dad got a call from a man making children's TV programmes. Even Mum laughed when she saw Dad on TV for the first time, dressed as a tomato.

"He's good though, isn't he?" she said proudly.

Well, the rest, as they say, is history. Everyone's heard of Dad now, but we still have the best Christmasses in the world. I wish we didn't have to have them on the yacht, though, because it turns out that the only one of us who really gets seasick ... is me!

Awful Uncle Angus

The ladies who lived at Laburnum Cottage liked things to be just so. They had tea-cups with roses on them, and plates to match, and embroidered napkins that they brought out for very special guests. (Ordinary people got paper ones, but they still had roses on them.)

The ladies were looked after by Mr. and Mrs. Meechum. Mrs. Meechum kept the house spick and span. Mr. Meechum did the garden. Both of them were saints in a way. No one was as fussy and finickety as Miss Julia and Miss Maria.

"Surely you're not going to plant begonias there, Mr. Meechum?" Miss Julia would say. "Dear me, it will look like a municipal park. Do try to think, please."

Mrs. Meechum was constantly being criticized for the thickness of her pastry and the dust on the little twiddly bits of the stairs. Miss Maria had been

known to take a magnifying glass to the windows in her search for specks after Mrs. Meechum had slaved all day to make them sparkle.

"They're so high and mighty," Mrs. Meechum moaned to her husband one day, when Miss Maria had lectured her for an hour and a half on the proper way to dust delicate ornaments. "And they're so perfect. I bet there are no skeletons in *their* cupboards. But how I would love to find they had some deep, dark secret!"

As a matter of fact, the ladies did have a deep, dark secret. It was one that they were desperate to prevent their friends from discovering. His name was Uncle Angus and he was, in the ladies' eyes, unutterably awful.

Uncle Angus was the ladies' late lamented mother's youngest brother. He had always been wild. As little girls, Julia and Maria shuddered at stories about their awful uncle. They heard how he had ridden his horse down the centre of the huge dining table at their grandmother's

house. They screeched at his mouse-eating contests with other boys. They trembled when they heard that he had once climbed the highest mountain in Tibet wearing only his socks. Uncle Angus certainly wasn't the kind of person who could be a good influence on two well-brought-up young ladies.

As Julia and Maria grew older, the refinement of their upbringing did them no favours. At the dances they went to as young women, no young man ever seemed good enough for either of them.

"Of course, he's good looking and he has a title," Julia said of the eligible Lord Cudlip, "but have you seen how he eats his peas?"

"The Earl of Blancmange is just as bad," Maria replied, with her nose in the air. "He has three castles and an estate in Australia, but he's never heard of Mozart."

And so the ladies became older, and the young men became married, and soon there was no one left for Miss Julia and Miss Maria at all. Living by themselves, with enough money to indulge themselves but not enough to live in high style, they became ever more prim and proper—and ever more scandalized by reports of the dreadful deeds of awful Uncle Angus.

When Uncle Angus invited his nieces to stay, they politely declined, but agreed to visit him for the afternoon. Miss Julia in particular refused to linger longer.

"I have no great conviction that his beds will aired," she said. "I will not risk my health for a scoundrel."

Now until this point, neither Miss Julia nor Miss Maria had ever set eyes on their uncle. Everything they knew of him was from newspaper reports or the shocked face of their mother when she heard yet another disgraceful story about her youngest brother. But despite expecting the worst, nothing had prepared these two delicately nurtured ladies for the extraordinary aspect of Uncle Angus.

For one thing, he was showing his knees! They were big, hairy knees, which made matters worse, as far as the ladies were concerned. Uncle Angus was dressed in a kilt, patterned socks as hairy as his knees, and huge boots.

"I don't understand it," hissed Miss Julia to her sister. "It's not as if he has anything to *do* with Scotland."

"It's probably easier to slip out of a kilt than trousers for all his, you know, *naked* activities," said Miss Maria darkly, which made Miss Julia squeal as if Uncle Angus was about to throw off his clothes there and then.

Uncle Angus did nothing of the kind. In fact, he seemed remarkably fully clad for July. He welcomed his nieces by clasping them to his chest in a bear hug, leaving the ladies dishevelled and shocked. For one thing, they were not used to being hugged by *men*! For another, they had come nose to hair with his awful, smelly beard, which appeared to retain the remnants of several days' meals.

"Thank goodness we didn't agree to stay the night," Miss Julia said later. "I

know for sure that he has kippers for breakfast. How anyone can eat fish that smell like *that* I can't imagine."

Nothing about Uncle Angus made the ladies want to visit him again. They rushed off at the first opportunity.

"I suspect, you know," said Miss Maria, "that he is quite, quite mad. I think he should be *seen*."

The ladies got in touch with Social Services and described an aged man, barely able to care for himself, living alone and in need of help. A young woman was sent round to make an assessment, only to leave rather smartly when Uncle Angus gave her a piece of his mind. Whatever he said to her—and from the colour of her face as she left some of it must have been rather rude—she was in no doubt of his mental or physical competence.

"That man is perfectly able to live an independent life," she told her colleagues, "and the longer it is before we have to have anything to do with him, the better."

Meanwhile, awful Uncle Angus had begun to send his nieces postcards. It seemed that he had bought a boat and taken himself off on an around-the-world adventure. His messages about dusky maidens and the unimportance of clothes in the tropics, sent the ladies into a decline. What if the postman read the dreadful drivellings? Worse still, what if Mr. and Mrs. Meechum saw them?

For weeks, the ladies got up at the crack of dawn to catch the postman before the Meechums could see what he brought. There were several more questionable communications from Uncle Angus. One mentioned that he had been at a feast where a local warrior had been eaten.

Miss Julia fainted to the floor on the spot (but was careful to land on a soft bit of carpet).

"We've got an uncle who's a cannibal," she murmured in a daze. "What

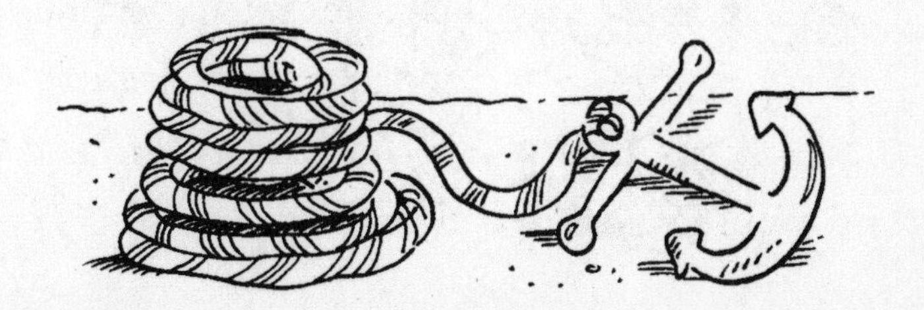

would we do if our neighbours got to hear of it? We could never attend the Ladies' Golf Club Luncheon again."

Fortunately, it was not long after this that Uncle Angus returned from his voyages. The ladies were able to relax a little now that it was unlikely that the postman would bring any more perilous postcards. But one morning, Miss Julia had a sudden and ghastly thought.

"My dear," she said to her sister in a whisper, for Mrs. Meechum was polishing

nearby, "what if he decides to visit *us*? If he can travel around the world all by himself, a matter of a few hundred miles isn't likely to stop him."

Miss Maria looked horrified.

"We can't have him here," she said. "Let's tell him we've got a dreadful disease or something."

"I will *not* claim to have a dreadful disease," replied Miss Julia sharply, "but what if we said that *we* were travelling around the world? That would stop him coming, wouldn't it?"

"But won't he expect us to send *him* postcards?" asked her sister.

"Not," said Miss Julia, "if we say we are travelling in deepest, darkest … er … Outer Mongolia."

But Uncle Angus had a new friend and seemed very little interested when he heard of the ladies' impending journey.

"I can't travel with old Bonzo," he wrote on a scruffy bit of paper that looked as if it might have been used for wrapping fish and chips. "He's almost as old as I am (in dog years) and he seems to have adopted me. I like having someone to look after. We make a good team."

"The man is blethering again," said Miss Julia. "He's taken up with some slathering hound who leaves hairs all over the furniture and slobbers on your slippers. Ugh! I can't think of anything worse. Can you?"

Miss Maria agreed.

"Uncle Angus's house is already the hairiest place I know," she said. "I'm not surprised he's taken up with a dog."

Miss Julia and Miss Maria discussed whether they should pursue their mock voyage to Outer Mongolia. In the end, they decided that the pretence was not necessary, as long as Uncle Angus was confined to base with his new friend.

But poor Bonzo did not enjoy his new home for long. One morning, reading the paper, Miss Maria let out a squawk.

"That dreadful dog has died," she said, "and Uncle Angus has been daft enough to put it in the paper! Look: 'Gone but not forgotten, beloved Bonzo, great companion of Angus Smith.' Is there no end to the man's idiocy?"

Well, no, there wasn't. The next news of Uncle Angus that reached Miss Julia and Miss Maria was also, sadly, in the paper. It seemed that he had been arrested for throwing peanuts at passers-by from the windows of his house. Why he should want to do such a thing, no one could discover, but once again he was found to be of (otherwise) sound mind. The magistrate sent him home with a warning.

Miss Maria fanned herself with the paper to regain her composure.

"I bless the day that dear mother changed our name to Smythe," she said. "No one, surely, will connect us with that exasperating man?"

Miss Julia agreed that all appeared to be well.

"If necessary, we shall just have to revive our Outer Mongolian trip," she said, "but I hope it won't come to that. To

think that we almost had a relative who went to *prison*!"

No more was heard from Uncle Angus for several months, although Miss Julia scanned the more sensational papers regularly to make sure he wasn't up to no good (and learnt many extraordinary things in the process).

Then, one evening, the telephone rang. It was a hospital the ladies had never heard of, and it seemed that Uncle Angus was a patient and not at all well.

"We believe that you are his nearest relatives," said a nurse. "We really think that if you want to see him, you should come at once. He doesn't have long."

It took Miss Julia and Miss Maria about two and a half seconds to decide that it would be unwise to tire poor Uncle Angus by visiting him. He would be better off ending his days in peace—alone.

But Uncle Angus was remarkably slow in ending his days. When, three weeks later, he was still lingering, the ladies decided that after all they should go to see him. It had occurred to them that he might be considering the need for somewhere comfortable for his convalescence. They were most anxious that he should be made to understand that their own cosy cottage would be quite unsuitable. It was a task they needed to do themselves.

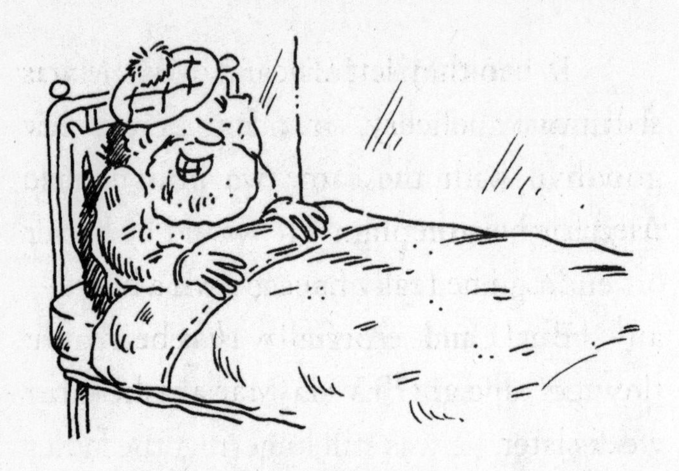

Uncle Angus, sitting up in bed in his tam-o'-shanter seemed pleased to see his visitors. When he heard what they had to say, however, his face darkened.

"I was looking forward to getting out of here," he said, "but now I'm not sure I'll bother. The food's not bad and the nurses are pretty. It would be fine if they didn't keep insisting I wash my beard. The idea! This beard hasn't been washed since the day I grew it at the age of eight. There's history in this beard."

The ladies didn't doubt it.

When they left Uncle Angus, he was still fairly cheery, but he didn't say goodbye with the same warmth he had used for his greetings.

"Can he really have grown a beard—any beard, and especially *that* beard—at the age of eight?" Miss Maria asked her elder sister.

"The ways of men are mysterious," replied Miss Julia. "It is best not to know."

The ways of Uncle Angus were certainly mysterious. Two minutes after the ladies left, he put his tam-o'-shanter on the bedside table and quietly died. When the news reached the ladies, they agreed that it was for the best really. He was old and ill, and his beard was a health hazard.

Life in the ladies' little cottage went on peacefully as before. They certainly did not miss Uncle Angus, and when they heard that he had been buried next to

Bonzo, they simply tut-tutted and went on pouring tea.

It was almost a month later that the letter came. It was an important-looking letter, on thick cream paper, and it bore the name of the famous firm of Umbleshanks and Peabody, solicitors to the rich and famous. Miss Maria brought it to her sister.

"I do hope it isn't anything at all unpleasant," she said. "I never feel that much good can come from solicitors."

But Miss Maria was wrong. The letter formally invited the ladies to the reading of the late Angus Smith's will. They might, it said, learn something to their advantage.

"But he didn't have any money!" cried Miss Julia. "Anyone could see that! You wouldn't live in the state he did if you had two ha'pennies to rub together."

Her sister agreed.

"Still," she said, "we may as well go. Who knows? Perhaps he had a piece of family silver tucked under the bed or something. We are his only living relatives, so he will have left us everything he has."

It was exciting entering the sobre regions of the Umbleshanks and Peabody offices. The ladies waded through thick, green carpets and sat down on highly polished furniture. It was young Mr. Peabody himself (grandson of the founder) who invited them into his office and offered them tea.

"I have to tell you," he said, glancing down at his notes, "that your uncle left a substantial amount of money. Were you close at all?"

The ladies sat dumbfounded for a moment. Then first Julia and then Maria suddenly realized that they had, indeed, been exceptionally close to their uncle. They pulled out delicate handkerchiefs and sobbed in a ladylike manner but not so loud that they couldn't hear what the solicitor was saying. For what he was saying was very interesting indeed.

"The estate in total comes to around half a million," he said, "and your uncle was very clear about his wishes."

The ladies sobbed more softly and strained their ears.

"If he has left us just a little something to remember him by," sniffed Miss Julia, "that will help to ease our sorrow a little bit. We miss him so much."

"It seems that your uncle guessed that would be the case," smiled the solicitor. "He has indeed left you just a little something. It's a picture frame, with a photograph of himself and his great friend Bonzo inside."

There was a long pause. The ladies waited. The solicitor smiled.

"And…" prompted Miss Julia.

"And the remainder of his estate, amounting, as I said, to just over half a million, goes to found the Bonzo Smith

Home for Abandoned Dogs," said Mr. Peabody. "A charming gesture, I'm sure you agree."

Miss Julia and Miss Maria felt tempted to deliver themselves of some quite unladylike language. Instead, they suggested forcibly that Uncle Angus had not been in his right mind when he made the will.

"Let me see," said Mr. Peabody, "it was just after someone—why, you yourselves, ladies—insisted on having him assessed. No, you need have no worries on that score."

The ladies took their leave.